MW01601644

THE DIANA STRAIN SERIES

THE
DIANA
STRAIN

JOSHUA CONVERSE

Copyright © 2020 Joshua Converse. All rights reserved.
Printed in the United States of America. No part of this book
may be used or reproduced in any manner whatsoever without
written permission except in the case of brief quotations embod-
ied in critical articles or reviews. For information:
https://joshuaconverse.wixsite.com/joshuaconverseauthor/contact

Cover Photo by Brian Mack
Cover Design by Carrie Glenn
All rights reserved.

ISBN: 979-8690450762

DEDICATION

For Bram.

CONTENTS

ACKNOWLEDGMENTS

The author gratefully acknowledges his first readers, particularly Guy Swalm, David Villani, Elle Otero, his long-suffering wife Amy, Professor Henry Marchand, the Creative Writing Program at Monterey Peninsula College, Richard Hellam (who endured a reading very outside his usual fare but whose time in the backcountry of Big Sur contributed to the work immensely), his editor Carrie Glenn, and all readers whose patience and insight that brought this novella into being. All errors are my own.

CHAPTER 1

HUNTER AND MADISON
BREAK DOWN

Friday night
One night before Full Moon
20 May, 2016

O n Friday, the near full moon rose over the Big Sur coastline bringing with it a pale, cold second daylight. Far below the high cliffs, in the frigid and shark haunted Pacific, there shimmered a glittering ribbon of a pale, cold twin of the moon surfacing from the deep. Highway One slid south, dark as an oil spot, along and bestride the rolling hills to the East, bisecting them from the cliffs, rocky shoals, foaming waves and beaches to the West. Fingers of fog crept across the highway, slow and languid, obscuring the stars and diffusing the moonlight.

Then, headlights.

The low whine of an engine struggling up a hill, sizzling and hissing and spitting. The sedan rolled to a stop on the shoulder just before Bixby Bridge, and the man and the woman inside looked at each other with something like concern. It was early yet, but the highway was silent and deserted. Often there were people at this lookout taking in the view through their cell phones, or photographers fussing with tripods, but tonight there was no one to help them. The young man stepped out and opened the hood, cursing, as steam hissed and bellowed into his face and up to join the thickening fog, coolant splattered over the dust and gravel, pooling beneath the Prius.

"Shit," he said, staring at the hemorrhaging guts of his car without much of an idea what he was actually looking at. He was in his early twenties, well-built but a bit slight, with longish curly hair beneath a striped knit skullcap. He sported a close-cropped and spotty Van Dyke on his face and a heavy-gauge earring in each ear. He pulled out his cell and lifted it high like an idol. Hands up, he stalked between the cliff edge and the highway's first yellow line. Then said, "Shit," again with feeling.

"No service?" asked the woman from the passenger side, coming around to the car's hood. She was waifishly pretty with short brown hair and blue eyes. Her nose was dappled with small freckles, and she wore a newly-bought red and black checkered flannel shirt.

"Nothing," he said. "I'm changing services. Seriously. Sprint is shit."

She pulled out her own cell and frowned. "Probably these hills," she said.

"Well, uh…shit," he said, scratching his head, looking from useless phone to useless vehicle like a man trying to extrapolate particle Physics from a mote of dust and failing. He sidled over to the cliff's edge again and looked out on the ocean, even as obscuring mist like a wall began to fly up and over him, rolling into the hills beyond.

"Hunter, I bet someone will come along and we can call for a tow from the hotel," she called, looking into the guts of the car, using her cell as a flashlight.

"Yeah," he said turning. "You're probably—"

Something darker than the night around it moved across the road, near the far edge of the bridge. Something large.

"What is it?" she asked, looking up at him, then, noting the direction of his gaze and his slightly nervous expression, she turned and looked at the bridge.

"I thought I saw something."

"Like what?"

"I don't know. An animal, maybe."

"Are there bears here?" she asked, her voice rising into a moderately higher register. He said nothing, squinting into the fog-thickened moonlight across the empty highway.

"Hunter, are there *bears*?"

"I don't *know*, Madison. Let's just get back in the car, okay?"

He couldn't have explained why he was trembling suddenly and dampening with sweat, but whatever that shadow or barely discernible silhouette, it had triggered something primal, something near panic in the back of his modern man's primitive brain. They got back into the car, slamming the doors and locking them. They both pulled out their phones with the same movement and with identical expressions of hope and frustration.

"Shit," he said.

She looked at him with mild irritation, then back to her phone, even as the billowing fog enveloped the car.

"Maybe we should—" she suddenly stopped short, as if someone had poured ice water down her back. Her body jerked, then clenched without her permission, and she dropped her phone.

"What is it?" he said quietly but with mounting fear.

"Something. Something in the fog. I thought I saw it... just for a second. It was big."

They had left the hood up and could only look out their windows as the fog thickened further around their little car.

"If it's a bear, it'll just go away and leave us alone. There's no food in the car," he said.

"There's that kombucha you just *had* to have," she said, looking at the bottle in the drink holder.

"Bears don't like kombucha, Madison, Oh my God, seriously?"

"Well I don't know, Hunter. I'm scared," she said shrilly.

"Okay, okay, just be quiet, okay? We don't want it to—"

There was a slow, deliberate scratching on the roof of the Prius, and then a heavy thud as of something jumping, then settling on top of the car. They both slid down in their seats involuntarily.

"What's happening?" he whispered.

"Ohmygod."

An inhuman growl so deep and guttural it positively shook the car and made her clap her hands over her ears. Then one of the doors was ripped off the hinges with a shriek of twisting metal and shattering plastic. They both screamed. Then long claws shot down from the car's roof, and Madison was thrown out of the vehicle and over it, pulled by the neck, which gave with a wet snap; her scream was cut short. Her body was a limp, dark shape on the darker highway outside his window.

Hunter was running then, not looking back, screaming and keening into the night but barely aware it was his own voice in his ears. He fell twice, slashing his knees on the gravel before he gained the bridge, not daring to look back. He had shat himself but was not aware of it. Hunter heard something like iron nails skittering on asphalt, then a tearing, wrenching roar. Something landed on him. Blearily, he thought at first that he had been hit by a truck, but it was something huge and snarling and darker than the night. He felt a hairy, bloody claw, hot and unbelievably strong close around his throat, and then there were jaws on his scalp, and before the intense pressure of the bite crushed his skull like a walnut in a hydraulic press, he smelled the charnel stink of its breath and screamed.

Then he did not scream.

Then he was gone.

CHAPTER 2

FRANK GETS A CALL

Saturday morning
Day of Full Moon
21 May, 2016

Frank had been dreaming the dream again when the phone rang. He swam up from sleep and, still in darkness, pulled the rotary phone off its cradle.

"Yeah?"

"Frank? It's Stella. Need you to come in. Something on the Highway down by Bixby Bridge. Couple kids dead."

"Yeah," he said. "Be there in a bit."

"Thanks," she said and hung up.

Frank reached for Lela in the dark, found the softness of her shoulder, rolled over and kissed it, then slipped slowly and quietly out of bed, grabbing a handful of clothes from the chair by the door, and stepping out into the hall.

The bathroom clock said 0415. He relieved himself, washed, shaved, and dressed, then went to the kitchen for that vital first cup of coffee. Once in his truck, cruising south on Highway One through the peanut-butter-thick fog, he allowed himself two cigarettes. He saw the scene as a dome of light well before he got to it, the red and blue lights swirling crazily against the cliffs and bouncing madly off the pale fog as he followed the highway's extremity out over the edges of the hillsides.

The Highway was not closed but had been reduced to one lane with an officer some hundred yards from the bridge at either end. The officer at the north end waved him through.

"Mornin' Frank," he said.

"Mornin' Brian," said Frank, steering his way to the shoulder so he could walk the rest of the way in.

There were two ambulances, the Coroner's van, and six or seven black and whites. There was the familiar feeling of an early morning crime-scene, and Frank realized he could go for months without thinking about it, but when he got back into a scene like this, he had missed it. He liked the order of it, he supposed, or trying to make sense of chaos, or something even more complex that he didn't care to hazard a guess about. Introspection was not his long suit.

As he approached, the officer in charge (*Jones? Carlson? Carlson. That was it…*) waved him over to a powder blue Prius, tinged red in the lights. The fog was still thick, but he could make out a clot of men in the middle of

Bixby Creek Bridge, as well. A forensics team was collecting samples from the far lane where it appeared a body had landed, and on the other side on the lip of the cliff, was the crumpled, smashed door of the Prius.

"Hit and run?" asked Frank.

"Don't think so," said Carlson. "I'd think some kind of animal attack, but damned if I know what it was. Two kids. Hunter Shaw and Madison Blakely, both out of Marin, according to their licenses. Same address. Vehicle's registered to him. Looks like it overheated, blew a seal, and while they were waiting for somebody to come by, something came along and jumped on the car, scratched up the roof, ripped the door off…"

"Then grabs her, throws her out, he runs, and it gets him on the Bridge," said Frank.

"That's how it looks," said Carlson. "Her neck is broken, at the very least, and his skull was crushed by a bite."

Frank whistled appreciatively, "Bear, maybe?"

"Yeah, maybe. Never heard of a bear doing anything like this, particularly unprovoked."

"Could be rabid," said Frank.

"I mean, could be, but…" Carlson looked back over the cliff. "Aren't rabid animals afraid of water? Why would it come down here?"

Frank nodded, then walked over to the car. He pulled out a penlight and examined the scratch marks on the top of the Prius. They were big—but not Grizzly bear big. He looked down at the twisted hinges of the passenger door. Whatever had done it was unimaginably powerful. It had snatched her out of the seat, probably snapping her neck in the process, then it picked her up and threw her up and over, across the car toward the highway. Why?

Frank walked over to the door where it lay at the cliff's edge. It had shattered the window, but there were very clearly scratch marks on the handle of the door itself. It had ripped the door off its hinges with, it appeared by the cleanness of the break, one mighty jerk. This had pulled the handle itself out of shape and bowed the whole door outward—

But it had used *the handle*.

Frank cocked his head and looked over the scratched door handle. Five scratches. Four in a rough line, and one at an angle. A thumb?

He stood and walked over to where the body had lain. A small pool of blood and viscera remained and no more. Likely they'd loaded her into the Coroner's van. He walked up the bridge, pen light sweeping over the ground. He reached a knot of men who were still clearing away what remained of Hunter.

"What happened here, Phil?" he asked the Coroner.

"Whatever it was ate him. Or, parts of him. Brain. Liver. Pancreas, maybe? I'll have to do an autopsy to be sure, but it looks like it was after specific, rich organs."

"And the girl?" Frank asked.

"Same."

"How big was this thing, Phil?"

"If I had to guess? Big. Bite radius was huge. At least three hundred pounds, maybe nine feet."

Frank looked into the dark, bloody mess congealing on the cold concrete of the bridge and turned away, walking in a slow circle around the body. He found what he was looking for in a bloody paw print ten feet from the body, then another. Then another. On two legs. Heading south. At the edge of the bridge, it moved off into soft dirt and then southeast into the hills where the bloody paw prints gave way to faint, damp impressions, and on top of the little hill overlooking Highway One, the tracks disappeared entirely among the rocks.

Frank stood there in the quiet for a long time, looking not at the sea but into the dark interior of highlands beyond, where something murderous loped under the failing moonlight.

CHAPTER 3

THE SHIFTING GROUND

Saturday
21 May, 2016

That afternoon, traffic passed back and forth on Bixby Creek Bridge oblivious of the carnage the night before, and if blood remained as a slowly blackening stain in the daylight, the few who noticed gave it no more thought than they might of the occasional dead raccoon or skunk on the side of the road. The day had turned muggy and warm, and farther out to sea, clouds stirred and coalesced out beyond the rolling fog bank on the horizon.

The infamous wildfires of California had set their hot tongues over the hillsides and scrublands of Big Sur the summer before, certain patches overlooking Highway One were still blackened and burned; devoid of yellow foxtails, bare of scrub oak and Monterey pine.

By late afternoon, black thunderheads cast themselves over the coastline like the draped bodies of pagan supplicants over some ancient altar, and there began, despite the 50-year drought, a hard rain.

Miles south in Big Sur proper, *The Cauldron* was Big Sur's only occult supply shop/bookstore. It was situated adjacent to the Big Sur River Inn (spitting distance to the Big Sur River itself, which was, on most days, more like a cool and pleasant creek in this spot) and precisely next door to *The Pale Maiden Publick House*.

The owner of *The Cauldron*, known only as Nob, looked up from his paper as the rain began to pound the cement parking lot outside.

Down on his paper, the news was bad: a couple had been killed on the road last night by Bixby Creek Bridge, maybe by a bear or a mountain lion. Very unusual animal behavior, possibly the result of rabies, claimed the *Monterey Herald*. Nob, however, suspected a rarer disease still.

He rose, a towering man of seven feet, unfolding from his chair just as lightning flashed and thunder rattled the rain-lashed panes. He walked to one of the large bay windows at the front of the shop and looked out; already the river looked fuller. It was an unusually grand storm and would last late into the night. He wondered what such a storm portended. It would be a moment, and a question, he would remember for some time to come.

Ten miles north of *The Cauldron*, a muddy hillside blackened by summer flames now began, under the tender ministrations of pounding rain, slowly to lean over Highway One like a nightmare witch over the bed of a sleeping child. By dusk, the first layer of topsoil had seeped down to the shoulder, and by midnight, the hillside had leaned too far over the road and into the Pacific. Finally, twenty tons of dirt and rock fell from both above and below the highway. The road gave way for a hundred yards in both directions, then plummeted crashing and groaning, echoed by the thunder, two hundred yards into an angry white foam sea lit only by flickering tongues of lightning.

The road was out. Big Sur was cut off from the Monterey Peninsula to the north. The mountains hemmed the east. Thirty miles to the south, another black and fire-raked hill began to groan and lean over Highway One. By dawn on Sunday, there was no way to get to Big Sur by car and no road out.

CHAPTER 4:
JAWS AND TEETH

"This was no boat accident." –Matt Hooper, *Jaws*
Sunday
22 May, 2016

Sunday afternoon at about four o'clock, when the storm finally cleared, Blake and Mira went out to Pfeiffer State Beach with their surfboards, knowing (or hoping) the storm had churned up the waves. They paddled out past the high, heavy breakers about fifty feet apart and began to time the swells, awaiting their chance. The waves were high, the surf powerful, and they rode what they referred to as "epic waves" from swell to shore, over and over again.

What Mira and Blake did not know (though they had resigned themselves to it long ago) was that they were not alone in the water. A great white shark had come in from the deeper depths. She had, in fact, cruised down from the Farallones overnight while the storm wheeled above her.

She watched the two surfers for a half hour that afternoon, gliding by beneath their feet, circling in wide, lazy elliptical orbits through the murky green water. She was one of what researchers at the Farallones, if they could have told Mira and Blake, called "The Sisters," a group of truly enormous females that ruled this part of the Pacific. From nose to tail—had one the temerity to take her measure—she was twenty feet long and as big around as the VW bus in which Mira and Blake had come to Pfeiffer.

She circled them in ever closer, ever sharper circles, growing agitated at their disjointed, flailing movements in the water, so like a fish in distress that the primitive brain clicked over, at some nebulous, unmarked point, from investigation to predation. She chose the smaller of the two, the one who smelled more sharply in her nose, and when Mira paddled out to the next swell, her hand came within inches of brushing the Sister's dorsal fin but did not. Then the surfer caught her wave, and the shark followed, a flick of her tail powerful enough to overtake board and body.

And yet.

And yet.

This time Mira rode the board all the way to the beach and skidded to a halt just in front of Blake as the light was waning behind her in one of the famous Pfeiffer State Beach sunsets. The Sister turned in frustration and patrolled languidly, parallel with the shore.

"We done for today?" asked Blake, reaching for her and finding her hips with his hands.

"I guess so," said Mira with a grin, standing up on tiptoe to kiss him. They were a handsome couple: she was darker skinned, a mixture of Polynesian, French, Mexican and Mestizo, with medium-length auburn hair bleached almost blonde in places by the sun. He was tall, well-muscled with broad shoulders and a narrow waist—nearly the California cliché surf god of Hollywood proverb; he only lacked the dialect, for he had never in his life referred to anything as "totally tubular."

They kissed for a long moment, hands roaming, before they both began to shiver and decided without words it was time to change out of their wetsuits, lay out a towel, smoke a joint or two on the beach in the fading light, and perhaps, then, to make love under starlight.

As they began to strip, Mira looked up absently at the tree line and froze.

"Blake."

"Yeah?"

"Blake…" she pointed to the copse of scrub oak not far away. "Something... eyes in the tree."

"Trees don't have eyes, dude," said Blake, pulling on a t-shirt that read "Impeach Hate: *MoveOn.org*," wadding the wetsuit up in a ball by his feet.

"No, Blake. *Look.*"

Something in her voice made him stop and look up, first to her pale, stricken face, then to the trees. In the last light of the day, he saw it.

Red eyes seethed in the shadows, too large to be a man's. And below those eyes were jaws with nearly luminous, perfectly white fangs leering out in a ghastly rictus of perfect malice.

"*Don't run,*" he said softly. "Let's. Just. Walk. Slowly. Back."

She breathed quietly for a moment then said, "Maybe it's a mask or something some kids put in the tr—"

But it moved, leaning forward into the light, an enormous wolf with the grotesquely clawed hands nearly like those of a man. On it came, loping out of the trees on its trunk-thick hind legs. A low growl escaped its throat as it scented their fear.

"When it comes," he said to her in a voice that was fighting a losing battle with panic, "get to the bus. I'll try to keep it busy."

She was going to protest but the words dried up in her mouth. Blake had leaned down to pick up his board, the only thing to hand, thinking perhaps to keep it between himself and the wolf thing. It came on, that pearly grin of menace on its terrible face.

It closed now, and Blake started forward, the board out lengthwise. Mira picked up hers as well and threw it at the beast, point forward, chest-high. It swiped the board away with ease and swept in close with its claws out—first opening Blake's joint at the shoulder then flaying his chest from shoulder to rib in a riot of bloody spray, then it followed with the other paw, slashing his neck and face, slicing his carotid artery in a rooster tail of red heat, lifting him from the ground with the force of the blow. Blake made a wet gurgling sound and landed convulsing in the sand, bleeding beside his reddened board. The wind rose on the beach then, and with it the smell of salt and blood.

Mira was already in motion. She gained the parking lot without knowing how she had done it, screaming and crying, and somehow got into the driver's seat of the VW bus. She turned the key and the engine rumbled to life, then she was skidding out of the parking lot, rolling over speed bumps at forty and throwing sparks from the front and rear bumpers as she did so. She hadn't meant to leave him, and she hadn't meant to run, but panic had taken hold. She screamed inside the car, and wept, and cursed, and just about when she got to the highway and resolved to go back with the baseball bat they kept in the rear, a heavy blow from the passenger side toppled the van over roughly onto its side. A horrible shearing of metal and the stinging shock of broken glass, and its face, frothing with rage, was straining down to meet her. She was dazed, having hit her head on the driver's side window—below her, had she known it, was a spider web of broken glass with a bloody spot in the middle. She screamed something beyond words or ideas, something from the depths of incoherent primal terror, or the wordless, bursting fear unknown since infancy; then its jaws found her throat, and there was nothing for Mira anymore.

Somewhere out beyond the shoreline, The Sister scented blood on the beach, and she turned with a sharp, agitated flick of her tail to disappear into the darkening green gloom of the Pacific night.

CHAPTER 5:

RANNULF BERSKR

"God save us from the fury of the North Men."
–Traditional English Prayer
Thor's Day
17 October, 837 A.D.

On a night bad for traveling, it was a feud that brought
Rannulf the Red to Freki's door. Freki lived in the
hills above a longhouse called Skirigssal. It sat on
the lip of a great forest where it was said trolls roamed
by night and, in the darkest patches, by day. The old
women in the nearest village said Freki had a blood re-
lation to the Aesir, the gods. Most of the warriors dismissed this as the sort of talk women get up to of a night
when there is no man to take them to bed.

It did not matter to Rannulf. What he did know was
that Freki could help him, and it was help he needed.
He had been insulted, and he would not bear it.

Sven, son of Torvald, had avenged old Torvald's death in honorable combat with Rannulf's cousin Hrolf Hammer-Hand. Sven had cut Hrolf open from balls to beating heart with one great slash of his sword, and that had been that. This would have been fair enough, but then Sven decided to kill two of Hrolf's brothers in a drunken brawl over whether Hrolf Hammer-Hand had died a coward. It wouldn't do. Rannulf would not bear the insult to his blood-kin and his clan and his name.

Unfortunately, Sven knew it, and he had retreated to the King's mead hall in Kristiania. It would be far too well-guarded, and it was very likely the ways were watched, and Sven would have men laying for him in the passes. Rannulf needed help, and he needed counsel, and if both were of the supernatural variety, so much the better. Sven's head had to come away from his shoulders, and that was fucking that. Rannulf did not intend to die in the doing of it.

It was the bitter end of the fall harvest, and the winds were high and bitterly cold when Rannulf had set out, in the darkest part of night, for Freki's house. He wanted no one to mark his going, and so took his time and crossed his own path back again. Even in his skins and cloak, the sleet chilled great Rannulf the Red, who had earned his name both on account of his flame-red hair and beard, and for the savage painting of his person with the blood of his enemies in battle—so great was the stroke of his axe that often he was a damp crimson very early into a melee. Rannulf climbed out of the valley with glacial deliberateness, crossed the scree by the light of a guttering torch, and waded the chill of a dark and nameless river, shivering and laughing to himself.

Freki appeared to be waiting for him outside of the little hut where he made his home, smoking a pipe. He was a small man with a high forehead and slightly pointed ears, a long, white-marbled braid down the middle of his back and a scar over one eye. The eye itself had clouded over like a pail of milk run through with blood.

"I am Rannulf the Red, son of Olav, son of Og, I have come to speak with you about revenge."

"I am Freki, and my father is dead, and his father is dead, and they cannot help me."

Rannulf eyed Freki uncertainly at this unusual, irreverent, slightly profane greeting. Freki chuckled, turned, and gestured his guest inside. Rannulf had to duck to come through the door. The hut was welcoming and warm, lit by a merry high fire in the hearth.

Freki gestured to a bench at a rough-hewn but clean table near the fire and sat down when Rannulf did, sucking at his pipe.

"Rannulf the Red, you say?" said Freki. "You're the one who won the swimming competition last year down in the village." It was not a question.

"Yes," said Rannulf.

"And you went a-Viking in your eighteenth summer with your father, is it not so?"

"It is so," said Rannulf.

"And you killed a bear once with a sword, I have heard it said."

"I did," said Rannulf.

Freki nodded twice up and down, more to himself than to Rannulf, as if satisfied on these points. "And now the warrior braves the chill of a particularly bad night of sleet and freezing rain, soaks his already-sodden leathers crossing a river so he can find my door three hours before dawn. Why?"

"I need a means of vengeance, but the man's clan is protecting him. I want his head. Just his."

"This man's name?"

"Sven, son of Tormund."

"That big lad? His clan is kin to the King."

"Yes," Rannulf said.

"And the King is a Christian," said Freki.

"So I've heard," said Rannulf.

A slow smile crossed Freki's lips, "I see. You'll cross clan and King for vengeance—this has almost gone out of style. These are the Old Ways."

"I hear you are a Gothi, a priest of the Aesir, maybe a scion of their bloodline. I need your help."

"The Christians have supplanted the Gothi. Their church in Rome holds the power now. Their God is the one the people pray to," said Freki lightly.

"But that God is not going to help me with my revenge, and I will have it."

Freki's smile widened, showing his four teeth, unevenly rooted in his mouth.

"I'll have three oaths from you, Rannulf the Red, and given these three oaths, I will help you."

"Name them."

"First, you must swear by spit that you will tell no one nor speak word ever of what passes here tonight or that you ever came."

Rannulf spat on his palm, "I swear."

"Second, you must swear by blood you will never return to me."

Rannulf ran his hand casually over the blade of his axe, squeezed his great hand into a fist and dripped blood on the floor.

"I swear."

Freki nodded.

"Third, you must swear by your soul you will kill Sven, son of Tormund, and... Do this in the sight of the Christian King."

Rannulf thought about this for a moment, then said, "I swear by my own soul."

Freki grinned at him and popped out of his chair with almost alarming energy and lithe grace for one so short and seemingly ancient.

"Strip," he said, moving to the back of the hut and through a small door, hauling out a bleating goat kid.

"Eh?" said Rannulf.

"I say strip. Take off your bloody clothes, Rannulf the Red," he said and laughed loudly, extraordinarily loudly and in high good humor.

Rannulf shrugged, wondering not for the first time if Freki was mad.

Freki had the kid tucked under one arm, though it struggled and could not escape, and pulled a long iron spike and a coil of rope from where they hung on the wall of the hut. The wind moaned outside, a mournful sound. Freki produced a dagger from his belt and stuck it between his teeth, then bustled outside. "Follow," he said around the dagger.

Rannulf, naked as a bold boast, followed the Gothi into the cold. Freki proceeded quickly, so quickly Rannulf had to hurry to catch up, bare as his feet were on the frigid, rocky ground. In the dark Rannulf could see little but what light the open door of the hut threw off some distance away, but Freki knew the land and at the very edge of the forest he staked down the bleating, crying kid, then ran the dagger over the beast's white fur at the ankles until blood came. Now it began to cry out even more shrilly and desperately, tugging at its bonds. Freki patted its head and said, "When the wolves come, kill one, Rannulf the Red."

"They come in packs," said Rannulf.

"Yes."

"I'm naked."

"Yes."

"Unarmed."

"Yes."

"Can't see."

"Yes."

Rannulf wondered, not for the first time, if Freki was mad, but said, after a moment, "Just one, then?"

"Just one, son of Olav."

It didn't take long; blood had been in the air minutes and there were howls met by other howls in the forest, coming closer. Freki walked, in no particular hurry despite the driving wind and freezing rain, back toward the hut and waited there beneath the eaves. Rannulf cast about, found a good-sized stone, big as a man's head, and climbed a tree near where the kid bleated and cried and kicked.

His eyes adjusted to the darkness, and the tree offered a little protection, though he shivered bitterly. And they came, as sure as moonlight. They were wary, so close to the old man's hut, but they smelled blood, and they were many—perhaps a dozen.

When the first great grey timber wolf, easily one of the largest he had ever seen, padded over to the prone goat, Rannulf tensed, readied, and hurled the rock with all his fury down on the beast's head. It fell like a hammer and landed squarely on the big wolf, mid-skull, and as it collapsed, dazed and half-unconscious, Rannulf followed, landing full force all knees and elbows on its throat and ribcage with a wrenching crunch. It yipped and whimpered and kicked, reflexively turning to bite, but its neck was broken—the others were startled, and drew back for an instant before closing in, growling and snarling and snapping as one. Rannulf was up as soon as he knew the first was dead. He picked up his rock in one hand, the kid (rope and all) in the other, and tossed them the goat, threatening with the stone cocked and ready to fire at the nearest wolf. The wolves, angry but obviously ravenous, set upon the kid and began to rip it apart as it screamed and keened high and bitter into the night.

Freki began to bang a hammer on an iron pot, screaming and yelling from the hut, and they scattered. Rannulf gasped as he realized in the time it had taken for him to climb the tree again, they had stripped the kid of flesh, cracked every bone for the marrow, and left almost nothing. Three wolves retreated to the tree line, and Freki said, "Quickly, the wolf. Bring it."

Rannulf jumped down, hoisted the dead wolf over his shoulder, and followed the old man inside, shivering, blue-lipped, bloody, and nearly numb.

What followed was stranger still. After soup and a time by the fire in dry blankets, Rannulf found Freki in the back behind the hut, working on a poultice. They skinned the wolf carefully and by dawn had a pelt stretched and drying by the fire. Freki spread this poultice into the stretched pelt.

"Come here, Rannulf, son of Olav, son of Og" said the old man to the exhausted warrior. Rannulf did.

Freki drew his dagger and cut a line, thin and shallow, but bloody, at the meeting of Rannulf's arms and shoulders.

"Wear the skin," said Freki.

Rannulf wondered, not for the last time, if the old man were mad, but he pulled the pelt over his shoulder.

"Now," said Freki, and gestured to a makeshift bed of boughs beneath the eaves of the hut. "Sleep."

And Rannulf, powerfully exhausted, slept. In his dreams, he was a man no more, but a beast on four legs, and the cold, clear morning after the rains was alive with the scent of deer, of bear, of elk, and of boar.

His jaws champed. His tongue lolled. His mouth slavered at these scents, and he thought he would burst, his belly tightening with the pleasure of it—that he could chase them all down and *kill them all* and devour them bite by bottomless bite.

Rannulf the Red dreamed he was a wolf, and when he awoke, a wolf he was.

CHAPTER 6:
FRANK AND LELA

Monday
23 May, 2016

Monday morning at dawn, Frank and Lela were sipping coffee across the table as the blue morning struggled against the fog and the pine forest shadows in the hills above Monterey. That dawn light streamed into their kitchen pale and ghostly, giving her terrycloth bathrobe an almost luminous quality. He was dressed in a suit and tie, anticipating a day of testimony for a pending case.

"You worried?" she asked, smiling across the table from him. After ten years of marriage, he never got over how beautiful she looked by the light of morning. Something like a tree after a storm, clean and good. She was dark eyed, with long dark hair and a gentle smile.

"Nah," said Frank. "Case is solid."

"All your cases are," she said, her lips crinkling wryly. "Don't you always get your man?"

He laughed, "Some more than others, I'm afraid. And that's the Mounties. Eh?"

"Oh, right," Lela said. "The Mounties. Of Scotland Yard."

"Precisely," he said.

"Well, so long as it's a court day, maybe I'll treat you to dinner, Detective," she said.

"Oh yeah? I don't know if you can afford me," said Frank. "I've got very expensive tastes, you know."

"Mmm, yes, I remember. Before we met, you drank Folgers Crystals and lived on Chef Boyardee."

"And bacon," he said.

"Right, who could forget?"

"Just want to make sure the record is clear," he said, sipping at the (admittedly better-tasting) fancy French Roast coffee Lela had not so much insisted on as subtly introduced to the household when they'd begun courting.

"How about you today? What's on for you librarian types? Sub-question: I've always wondered, do you have to do shushing warmups together? You know, as a group? Before you open? Inquiring minds want to know."

"In fact, we do. I knew a librarian who chose to forego the obligatory shushing stretches, and she sprained her tongue. Couldn't talk for a year. Gruesome. But now that I've told you, you can't tell another soul, or they'll find us both. You know how it is..." She dropped her voice into a stage whisper, "*There's a Library Mafia!*"

"Well, there's my next case," he said, rising and rinsing his coffee cup (chipped, stained, ancient, nonnegotiable, and naturally loathed by the lady of the house) and placing it into the drying rack.

She rose and kissed him on his way out the door, "Be safe."

"Always am."

"Don't mouth off to the judge." Another kiss.

"You never let me have any fun."

"Well, if you were home earlier nights..." she said.

"Be home by five. Then you can buy me my expensive fat burger and terrible beer. Who knows? You might get lucky."

"One of your redeeming qualities is how easy you are to get into bed," she said, and squeezed his bottom on the way upstairs to shower.

The phone rang. Frank took it from its cradle on the wall.

"Yeah?" said Frank.

"Good morning, Frank," said Ingalls, Detective Sergeant in charge of his section. "Why the hell don't you have a cell phone yet?" Ingalls was in his mid-twenties, and Frank was old enough to be his father. In fact, he'd been on the job longer than Ingalls had been on the planet. Nevertheless, Shaun Ingalls was a rising star in the Department and a good cop, and he'd carried off more than one or two high profile cases that had people figuring he'd be chief in another decade.

"Hate 'em," Frank said.

"It would make my life easier if you had one. You're the only guy I know who doesn't."

"Gives you a headache, Sarge?"

"Damn sure does," said Ingalls.

"Bonus," said Frank, deadpan.

"Another couple murdered down on Pfeiffer State Beach. Looks like animal attack. We can get you in by boat, since the road is out."

"The road is out? When did that happen? Also, I'm in court this morning. Paulson Case."

"Not Mr. Current Events this morning, eh Frank? Storm washed out Highway One north of Bixby Bridge last night. It's in *The Herald*."

"Don't read it. The news is always bad. Take the highway being out, for instance..." Frank said. "But I guess it's good we got some rain."

"Yeah, well, if you did read a paper now and then, maybe you'd also know that Jeremy Paulson died in jail last night. I don't think you'll have to testify this morning."

"What?" Frank's voice tensed, "What happened?"

"Cellmate killed him, looks like."

"Took six months to put this damn case together. God*damn* it. I…" he took a breath, exhaled, wished for a cigarette, but didn't reach for the pack in his pocket. Not in his wife's kitchen. "Okay. So, double homicide. Pfeiffer Beach."

"Head out to the Coast Guard pier. Got a boat waiting to take you and some forensics people down. Local deputies have the area cordoned off."

"How long?"

"Looks like yesterday. Early evening, maybe, is what they're guessing, but we won't know until we're down there."

"I'll be in touch," said Frank.

"Yeah. How? Get a damn cell phone. That's an order."

"Been an order for quite some time," said Frank.

"I mean, the world needs meter maids. Keep up your insubordinate rapacity."

"I love it when you use your Big Boy voice," said Frank. "I'll call when we're done with the scene. One of those forensics guys *undoubtedly* has one of those evil little devices."

"I'll be eager to hear. If this is an animal, it needs to be put down soon. That's four victims in two days."

"We'll see." Frank hung up. He jotted a note on the way out the door and stuck it beneath a magnet on the fridge: "Court canceled. Big Sur by boat. Another scene. Dinner still on."

CHAPTER 7

CROW'S WARNING

Monday
23 May, 2016

Monday at 9am, when Nob opened the shop, scooping up the paper in its plastic bag from the stoop and jangling the keys, he hadn't noticed them. It wasn't until the dry, harsh croak of a *"caw"* came scratching down at him that he turned and looked at the shingle above the door and saw three black crows peering down at him with unsettling intensity.

He turned and regarded them for a long moment, cocking his head.

"Oh yes?" he said, half to them and half to himself. They did not move but stared into him with eyes as dark as jet, sharp as obsidian.

He turned back and opened the door to *The Cauldron*, closing it softly behind him. It was a comfortable place, spacious and well-lit, with a long, low slung set of positively brimming book stacks that ran the length of the shop on both sides of a central alley ordered with tables and a long counter at the back. The counter was topped with various casting components, wands, crystals, dream catchers, tarot cards, divining rods, bundles of white sage, geodes, Bagua, I-Ching coins, statuettes of Kali, Ganesha, Buddha, Hotei, St. Michael treading down a great Dragon, Guardian Angels, amulets, potions, oils, feathers, essences, vials, tinctures, chicken bones, voodoo dolls, crosses Celtic and Roman Catholic, rosaries, prayer beads, mezuzahs, hanukkahs, ritual knives, pestles, mortars, semi-precious stone assortments polished to a gleam, and the like.

Nob's desk was at a rear corner of the shop, riotous to the point of avalanche with stacks of books, papers, parchments, quills, sealing wax; flotsam, ephemera, and detritus. In the very center of the shop was an enormous wrought iron cauldron seven feet in diameter and five feet deep, set into a large granite stone—a gift from his mother long ago. It had cost him as much as the down payment on the shop to ship it from Norway.

The Cauldron did a brisk trade among the Wiccans, New Agers, curious tourists looking for trippy dippy hippie novelty, white people who fancied themselves Indians, actual Indians (mostly from Southern Mexico), kitchen witches, surfers looking for protection from shark bite, recreational mushroom or LSD users turned "spiritual," kids looking to piss off their religious parents, the occasional Satanist down from San Francisco,

Catholics interested in Angelology or apocryphal Scriptures, academics of theology, sociology, and history, heathens, heretics, and seekers.

Nob had amassed, in the fifteen years he had been in business, a collection of books by order, discovery, and trade that was, in and of itself, rather remarkable. It ranged in scope from *The Gutenberg Bible* to original and subsequent editions of the *Malleus Maleficarum* (*The Witch's Hammer*) to the recently transcribed oral histories of the Hopi Indians to the complete works of Aleister Crowley, Anton Zander LaVey, and L. Ron Hubbard. People came from half the world away, sometimes, to find some obscure text or arcane tome, and yet it seemed there were always strangers coming in with packages and parcels (don't ask where they came from) to barter and trade.

It seemed to always have been his luck, wherever he found himself wandering in his youth, that Nob would find rare, unusual, and esoteric texts. They were somehow always affordable, even if there were nights he had to change his lodgings from a hotel in the Latin Quarter of Paris for a dirty hostel in the banlieues.

This morning, though, after the rains and in the cool light of such days, Nob was musing on the crows. He shrugged out of his ankle-length black duster, hanging it on the hat rack by the door. Three crows curled on his shingle, staring at him with identical looks of... what? Nob wasn't sure. Expectation, perhaps. Were they harbingers? Nob had seen things he could not explain, but he did not necessarily subscribe to every theory and superstition his merchandise might have suggested. Still. Their gaze felt ominous. A warning, perhaps.

Of...?

Nob put water on the boil in the kitchen at the back of the shop then poured himself tea when the kettle began to sing. He settled at an empty table in the central alley of the shop (he dared not sit at his desk for fear of being crushed by the disturbance and subsequent collapse of its towering piles). He opened his paper and read with slowly increasing alarm.

"Big Sur Cut Off by Landslide."

"Murder by Bixby Bridge Perhaps Rabid Animal."

He rose quickly and pulled a jangling velvet bag from a shelf and a flat, hard-baked red clay plate from behind the counter then brought them back to the table. He emptied the bag's supply of ox bone runes into his huge hand and then cast them onto the plate then gazed down at them in horror. He muttered a curse in his mother's tongue then hurriedly gathered the runes back into the bag and stuffed it into his pocket. He returned to the counter, replacing the clay plate there and reaching behind and beneath the counter for a snub-nosed .38 special and a plastic box of bullets, cast in silver.

He locked the door of *The Cauldron* hurriedly, then stiffened and turned, sensing their eyes on him. Three crows stared at him from his shingle with identical expressions of what he now knew was warning, but beyond them, the line of trees edging the parking lot on one side and the river on the other fairly drooped under the weight of several hundred black shapes in shadow, with eyes of gleaming jet.

"*Varulv*," he muttered and spat on the ground. "Odin be merciful."

CHAPTER 8

THE MISSING AND THE DEAD

Monday
23 May, 2016

Frank was regarding the overturned van on the road out of Pfeiffer State Beach. It didn't make sense. The forensics crew had fanned out over a crime scene that apparently spanned several hundred yards, from the beach where Blake Trezor had been all but vivisected to the road out where Mira Franklin had apparently fled for her life, only to have whatever it was *knock over the goddamn van.* Bears didn't do this.

"What do you think, Andy?"

Andy Parker, former deputy and investigator for the Monterey County Sheriff's Office, now working for the Park Rangers, was in his early 50s. He didn't look it, though, with his beanpole physique and placid, almost totally neutral expression. Frank knew better—Andy had a mind whirring behind those placid grey eyes that most people couldn't keep up with, just as they couldn't keep up with long-legged, rangy Andy on the trails of back-country Big Sur and into the Santa Lucia Mountains.

"Wasn't a bear. Wasn't a cougar. Wasn't a shark. And it wasn't Jack the Ripper," said Andy flatly.

"Well, then what the hell could do this?" asked Frank.

"Tracks we're pulling say it was an animal walking on two legs most of the time, non-retractable claws, five toed, opposable thumb on the forepaws. Preliminary measurements of the victims say bite radius of maybe twenty inches or more. Probably nine feet in length based on its stride, maybe more if there's a tail. Strong enough to knock down a rolling van at a blow. Means it can probably run as fast as a vehicle, at least at a stretch."

"So, a bear."

"Well, but bears don't have opposable thumbs, the biggest black bear I've ever seen doesn't have this kind of power, the grizzlies have been dead since the Spanish wiped them out hundreds of years ago, but even a rabid bear wouldn't do this."

"Because rabid animals are afraid of water, right?" said Frank, looking back down the road toward the beach.

"Right," said Andy, kneeling to look at the windshield of the van, spider webbed crazily with white, powdery cracks in the safety glass, but it was stained with black, congealing blood. There was almost nothing left to identify Mira Franklin, but her clothes and ID were in the back of the van along with Blake's. They were presuming identification, because her body, at least, wasn't going to provide much help. Her entire skull consisted of a few fragments of bone; whatever it was had apparently eaten the rest.

"There's another problem," Andy said, still looking at the windshield.

"What's that?" asked Frank, walking slowly around the van.

"There's a guard shack. This is a state park. There's supposed to be a ranger here during park hours, and sometimes there are patrols after hours, but the fellow who was supposed to be on duty yesterday evening never made it home. No sign of him in the guard shack at all. No jacket. No radio. Nothing. Like he never got here."

Frank frowned, "You have a ranger missing, too? You've searched the area?"

"We've started. After I got a call from his wife asking about him this morning when she woke up and he wasn't there, I got two teams of two looking in the surrounding area."

"What's his name?"

"John Abrams," said Andy, then he paused in thought. "I think," Andy began then hesitated. "I've heard of things like this, but never bought into any of it."

"How do you mean?" asked Frank.

"Well, we don't officially keep statistics on these things," said Andy, dropping his voice. "But around 1,600 people or so a year, I'd guess, go missing around national parks. That's every year. For state parks, it's probably a higher number—maybe a couple thousand, but mostly the brass keeps it under wraps, or it gets handled locally so the feds don't keep track. I've always figured it was people who trip and hit their heads, can't get up, and nature's cleanup crew handles the rest. Or they take a bad step and tumble into a ravine or a river. Nature's pretty unforgiving of mistakes. But I've heard people talk about other things. Things in the woods. Things that disappear people."

"What, Bigfoot?" Frank chuckled, but the seriousness on Andy's face startled him.

"I don't know. Like I said, I don't buy it, mostly, but this... what could do this to two strong young people? What would dare knock over a vehicle in motion and scoop out the woman inside and *devour her*? What could disappear an armed Ranger without so much as a drop of blood, radio, rig, and all? Family man, John is. Three kids. Wife. Been here fifteen years since he left the Marines. This kid didn't abandon his post or run out on his responsibilities. He's missing on the night this happened," said Andy. "And I'd wager he's likely in something's stomach. Boots, belt, and all... or there's a mind at work that's much smarter than a goddamn bear."

"Let's go take a look at the guard shack," said Frank. "And then we need to organize an official search and rescue for John."

They walked over to the guard shack.

"Looks like the van came in and they paid their fee around 4pm. John was here at that time," said Andy, looking at a clipboard hanging on a nail by the tiny wood shack's incoming traffic window. It was a tiny little structure with room enough for two chairs, two desks, and a radio charging unit fitted for four radios— only, there were just three radios on the charger.

No blood. Nothing broken.

"He never radioed for backup or help or to report he'd be out on foot?" asked Frank.

"No," said Andy.

Frank stepped out of the guard shack and looked at the bushes and trees beyond and the climbing hillside rising to the south not far away. Big Sur was a place where anyone could disappear, but if something was smart enough to make a park ranger disappear into thin air, why wouldn't it clean up after these attacks? Or had they just not found the other mess yet?

"I don't like this. Any of this," said Frank.

"You and me both," said Andy. "But we'd better beat the bushes."

"Call it in, I'm going to have a look around... but first…." he sighed then and picked up the phone in the guard shack. "I'd better call my wife." Dinner was off.

Nob walked into the Sheriff's Office substation in Big Sur and asked to see a calendar. The Desk Sergeant handed him a miniature "giveaway" calendar and Nob parsed it carefully.

"I need to see a list of missing persons for all of California around," Nob double-checked the calendar, "21 April, please."

The Desk Sergeant, whose name tag said "Adams," regarded him blankly. "Why?"

"I have my own reasons. This is public record, is it not?"

Adams frowned at this. "Yeah," he said, sliding off his chair, "I guess" he grumbled and walked toward the back of the room where a small monitor glowed like an unblinking eye. Adams, who looked perpetually bored and long-suffering, adjusted his girth in the chair and began to tap on the keyboard.

Then a scratchy voice came across the radio on the front desk where Nob waited, *"Central, this is Robert-Three, we need Search and Rescue out here by Pfeiffer State Beach to begin looking for John Abrams. Park Ranger went missing during his shift down here last night, over."*

Adams came back with an application and slid it across the desk, "Fill this out, and we'll have your information in the next few weeks," then, picking up the hand mic he said, "Robert-Three, this is Central, Roger that."

He looked up to ask the strange, tall man in a duster what his interest was in this list of missing persons, but the tall man was already gone. Adams shrugged and began Search and Rescue protocols.

CHAPTER 9:

THE DEATH OF SVEN TORMUNDSON

Freya's Day
December 23, 871 A.D.

The song had been merry in the High Mead Hall of King Ragnar Lodbrok despite the bitter snowstorm that raged outside, and Sven Tormundson was mightily drunk. On his throne at the high end of the Hall, the King dandled a maid on his lap, and she whispered to him and giggled and fawned over his beard and the gold of his adornments.

The King's Hall was full of courtiers and heralds and a few warriors—and while a young man might be expected to go a-Viking a few times before coming back home to play at court, few of those in attendance did it professionally. Sven was a warrior and accomplished in the trades of war and plunder. But there was a table near the great doors of the Hall where men with eyes of iron talked quietly, all but inaudible to any but each other in that place.

And these, Sven knew, were warriors who did not get drunk on mead and ale, whose hands were never far from axe, spear, and sword. Men whose brag, if brag they made, would shame even the King in his Hall. They were here in a bodyguarding capacity, and they drank little, and they said little.

Sven stood with the intention of going over to the table of warriors; he fancied himself of their kind and quality, and it was true he had a name even King Ragnar knew.

There were three great thudding knocks on the doors of the great Mead Hall, and the crowd quieted until only the howling wind outside could be heard.

"Who would travel on such a night?" asked King Ragnar, "Open my doors and admit the fool, if he can yet move for the frost." Hearty laughter and jeers erupted at this, and two of the warriors went to the high, wide doors. They were large enough to admit a team of oxen and a wagon, and each man pulled one of them open. Wind swept in icy and biting, guttering the fires in their braziers and dousing the torches. Standing there in a thick cloak was a tall figure, his beard emerging from the hood and cowl that hid his face.

"Enter, then," said one of the bodyguards, his hand on a hatchet hiding at the back of his belt.

"Sven Tormundson," said the figure, deep-voiced, unshivered, and unmoving.

Eyes fell on Sven; he did not so much see it as feel it, but the cold was clearing his head, and he stood, "I am Sven, Son of Tormund. What business is it you have with me, stranger?"

For a moment the figure said nothing, then he began to grow before their eyes, rising, spreading, and growling; the sound of joints ripping and tendons popping, bones breaking and re-breaking, knitting themselves back together and breaking further filled the Hall above the raging arctic winds. The warriors of the corner table drew steel: sword, spear, and axe. They came forward as one force while the rest of the Mead Hall stood there in paralyzed horror; the hood began to draw back, and the massive head and shoulders and bare torso of a wolf that stood as a man emerged.

In a voice as deep and cold as a glacier crevasse, the creature said, "I am Rannulf son of Olav, and I have slipped my skin to pay a blood debt to Sven Tormundson for the killing of my kinsmen. No one else needs to die this night, but I will have his heart between my jaws, even in the Hall of the King."

The first of the advancing warriors, side by side, bore their spears deep into Rannulf's flesh; one at his chest thrusting upward, and the other his groin at a downward angle, stretching him unnaturally. Two others, doughty men and tall, slid in close with drawn swords, one of them sweeping down in a fast, sharp stroke that sheared through Rannulf's right leg at the top of the thigh and sent it to the floor with a wet, thud.

The beast howled in rage and pain, furiously thrashing as the spearmen held him fast. The other swordsman came up, slashing for Rannulf's throat in a wide, glittering arc that would have removed his head from his neck. Rannulf pushed forward, further impaling himself on the spears, but giving himself room to duck and to close with the swordsman who had taken his leg, he snapped his jaws around the man's head and down to the shoulder, and jerked savagely. The suddenly limp bag of man-flesh under his jaws was instantly drenched in blood.

Rannulf snapped the haft of the spear and slashed low to high at the swordsman whose stroke had gone wide, rending from groin to lower jaw and sending the groinless, jawless corpse flying onto a nearby table, flat on its back. Two axe-bearing warriors who had not engaged swept in to flank him, one bringing the axe down squarely and deeply into Rannulf's back, forming a gash from kidney to kidney across the spine. Rannulf yelped, whimpered, growled—and the other axe man came in quickly, swinging for his arm, the bright blade neatly removed it at the shoulder, sparking on the stone floor.

Sven felt confident now, seeing the beast short an arm and a leg, bleeding and convulsing on the floor, and strode forward to perform the killing blow. Rannulf coiled as both axe men raised their blades again, and the swordsman slashed for his head. Then with explosive power he launched himself desperately at the enormous, flaming iron brazier in the center of the Hall, flipping the coals high and far into the straw thatching of the roof and wooden crags of the walls.

Sven, now paces away, stepped forward with a raised sword, but Rannulf snapped low with his great jaws, slicing from Achilles tendon to hamstring, and Sven fell—and before the warriors at the front of the Mead Hall could close, Rannulf had buried his snout seven inches into Sven's chest, feasting with monstrous hunger. The courtiers and heralds had fled into the icy night, the tables were overturned, and the roof was beginning to truly take flame now. The walls were smoking ominously like a fell vision of Ragnarok in miniature. The surviving warriors advanced grimly, weapons raised and ready.

King Ragnar regarded this as his Mead Hall burned, looked down at Rannulf, son of Olav, who had slipped his skin and traded it for that of a wolf to come even unto the Hall of the King to exact his blood price for kinsmen slain and wondered if such a beast were not best unleashed on his enemies.

The Viking warriors encircled the feasting wolfman and raised their weapons as one, preparing to pin Rannulf to the spot where he might burn in his own fire. The roof was beginning to come down in sizeable chunks and the fire roared against and above the swirling winds without.

"Do not kill him yet," said Ragnar the King, who somehow knew in his old bones the creature's wounds were not mortal. He stepped down, unperturbed by the flames, and strolled between his bodyguards, into the circle of steel that ringed Rannulf.

"Rannulf, son of Olav, you have exacted your blood price. Now, I can offer you other prizes…across the sea..."

Rannulf looked up from his meal and licked his bloody chops, his dark eyes full of malicious understanding. Already, his bleeding had stopped.

"Bring him with us," said the King, strolling to the door as the flames raged.

"Sire, your hall," said one of the warriors, "should he not die for the insult?"

The King turned slowly and regarded his man, unconcerned and as if he were in a garden and not the center of a hideous inferno roiled by a winter blizzard. "I can build another Mead Hall, but I cannot conscript another skinchanger, Lofi, son of Luz."

"Yes, sire," said the man, and roughly, the men half-carried the limping beast of out the mouth of the Hell that had been King's Mead Hall and into the frozen darkness of the blizzard.

"Let them resist me now," said King Ragnar, gazing to the West.

CHAPTER 10:
WORD GETS AROUND

Excerpted from the Monterey Herald, Evening Edition
Story picked up by USA Today
Tuesday
24 May, 2016

"Efforts continued today to locate Park Ranger John Abrams as Search and Rescue combed the area in and around Pfeiffer State Beach. Abrams had been stationed there on Sunday evening, but he appears to have disappeared entirely following a mysterious animal attack that left two local surfers dead at Pfeiffer that same evening. So far, no sign has been found of Abrams, 36, nor of the mysterious animal that police believe killed Blake Trezor, age 27, and Mira Franklin, age 25.

"Police officials have declined to comment on whether the attacks at Pfeiffer are likely related to the deaths of a couple on Bixby Creek Bridge.

Search and Rescue is always a challenge in Big Sur, which boasts some of the most rugged and remote wildlands in California. However, after Saturday's storm and the subsequent landslide on Highway One just a mile north of Bixby Creek Bridge, Big Sur has become even more inaccessible.

"Many locals worry about the upcoming summer tourist season, while others are simply wondering if they are trapped in the area while a dangerous animal is loose.

"Anita Moore, a local personality, artist, and Search and Rescue volunteer says, 'The truth is, things like this are going to happen more and more as we approach critical mass. Humanity has been trashing Mother Earth and the Sacred Oceans since we embraced Big Oil, and now the chickens are coming home to roost. Animals are going to fight back, aren't they? Can you blame them? Nature isn't going to put up with us just doing whatever we want for as long as we want. There will have to be an equal and opposite reaction, won't there? I tell you, this is only the beginning, until we can wean ourselves from the poisons being pushed by the corporations and the wealthy, things like these murders are going to keep happening. Prayers to the Great Spirit for the families, though.'

"Peter Gill, a former professor of Philosophy at UC Santa Cruz and owner of local watering hole and thirsty reporter's refuge *The Pale Maiden Publick House*, however, pontificated on a different perspective regarding these attacks, the landslides, and possible ramifications for Big Sur, 'We imagine our roads should stay as we build them. We're surprised when they fall down into the Pacific. We think that we are an apex predator, top of the food chain and, we're surprised when we are reminded that, the world is really subject to what Kipling called The Law of Claw and Fang. Humans think we have progressed or advanced beyond the rules of nature, the laws of entropy, and the flaws in our own plans. We fancy that our smart cars are really smart and make us smart, too.

'"On our best day, we're just a herd animal hiding in the trees until dawn. Sooner or later, whoever you are, you're "naked in the dark without a flashlight," to quote Wislawa Szymborska. The reason this is a news story at all is because people don't really believe their day (or civilization's) is coming, but it is. There are stranger things in Big Sur than are dreamed of in your philosophy, Ms. Mendoza. I wouldn't so much call it Judgment, as Reality intruding on our dreams.'"

CHAPTER 11:

A BAD HANGOVER

Tuesday Morning
24 May, 2016

Whatever had happened, Billy Hatfield's head was pounding, and his mouth tasted like something pungent had climbed right in and died a week ago. Billy opened one eye, as a test more than anything, and the light was an ice pick in the back of his head. He slammed his eyelid shut again and groaned. His throat was painfully raw, as if someone had rubbed turpentine into it with sandpaper. He was naked on his porch, he realized, as he began to shiver. At least, he hoped it was his porch. Then again, how could that be? The place he had rented was way out in the sticks. Hadn't he been in town? Where was his Cadillac? Had he walked?

Billy had moved to Big Sur from the Sierras near Tahoe to write over the summer and had rented this cabin in the backcountry. He had no smartphone, and there was no such thing as Wi-Fi out here; he had purchased an old Underwood typewriter and gone to work on his manuscript.

Friday night he'd decided to celebrate a good week of writing, hadn't he? He'd gone into town, bought a case of beer and stopped off at *Fernwood Tavern* for a pint and to watch some baseball. And then? Nothing. He remembered nothing. He risked opening his eye again and lolled his head over toward the driveway.

No friendly old drop top Cadillac there. Had he walked back? Gotten a ride? No answer came to his memory. Nothing stirred in the forest in the early morning but the sound of the birds. His head ached, and he looked down to take inventory. Black blood, cracked and old, covered his hands. His stomach threatened to heave up whatever it had. Billy slowly sat up and gasped for breath. The pain helped clear his head. He checked himself for cuts but found none, not even a scratch from wandering naked in the brambles or an errant bruise.

Whose blood, then?

Billy had the powerful urge to lick the black blood congealed on his hands and under his fingertips but slapped it down, horrified. He rose and thudded over the old boards of the porch, half-stumbling into the cabin.

In the entryway mirror, his face was a mask of black blood, dried and caked onto his face. The fancy analog alarm clock by his bed went off as he passed, and he picked it up as it sounded its klaxon. It said Tuesday. Not Saturday morning. He had lost three days? What had happened? Just what the hell had he done? He walked, trembling, to the bathroom shower, turned on the water and began to scrub someone else's blood away.

It was a long time before it was gone.

CHAPTER 12

THE PRIEST OF THE SWORD

4am
Tuesday
24 May, 2016

Father Giovanni Santa Ana awoke well before dawn in the rectory and slipped on his sweats and running shoes then headed into the bathroom, relieved himself, splashed cold water on his face, and went out into the cold spring morning. The San Francisco streets were all but deserted at this hour but for delivery trucks on their routes. He began to jog. He loped lightly north away from St. Peter's Rectory all the way up to North Beach to Saints Peter and Paul Church. He turned sharply, then, to the west and toward the Presidio, then south, until he passed Most Holy Redeemer and then Saint Philip the Apostle, and finally east again—thus completing a rectangle that bisected the city and took him back to the rectory.

This was a total of 10 miles or so. He checked his watch. 6am. An hour and forty minutes. Not bad. Not at all bad for a man in his forties. He cooled down outside his stoop as the first rays of morning crept over the city. Then he scooped up *USA Today* from the stoop of the rectory and went inside.

Back in his room, he flipped on the Today Show and did pushups, sit-ups, crunches, flutter kicks, and finally stretched. He went to the bathroom and showered in cold water. Set out his grain cereal with milk, a carafe of orange juice, and coffee as black and thick as pine pitch on the table by the window of his chamber, then spread the paper before him. A headline about the doings in Big Sur caught his eye, and he read with slowly building interest.

He went to the rotary phone on the bedside table and dialed then cradled the phone between his ear and shoulder and sat down on the neatly-made bed.

"Si, it is Father Giovanni. I need to speak to the Bishop today." He paused to listen, "I understand, but it needn't be long. I know he is busy."

The Bishop's assistant spoke, then Giovanni said, "It is a matter for the Order. An *auto-da-fé*. Yes. Very good. I will be there in an hour," he said and hung up.

Giovanni rose, smoothed the bed where he had sat on it and knelt there to pray for the souls of the afflicted and those in the grip of demons.

Later that morning, at the Diocese of San Francisco, Father Giovanni stood in the office of Bishop Michael Callahan with his copy of *USA Today* in hand.

"I would be very surprised," said the Bishop, "if this proves to be what you think it is, Father."

"I understand that, Your Excellency, but nevertheless, I am compelled to investigate by the vows of the Order."

"I understand membership in the Order of the Gladius Dei carries with it certain responsibilities and so I will give you leave to investigate, but you are *not* to call an *auto-da-fé* without consulting me, Father. The risk to the church is too great if you should be implicated in anything... extra-legal, however well-intentioned and however much it be in the service of Our Lord."

"Yes, Your Excellency," said Father Giovanni.

After a moment's pause, the Bishop turned away from the priest and regarded the street below, the city beyond.

"Tell me, Father, have you ever encountered a demon wolf?"

"Yes, Your Excellency. I have killed... several... in my time with the Order."

"It is, I understand, your specialty. Wolf hunting."

"Yes, Your Excellency."

"Rather an esoteric line of work, wouldn't you say?"

"It may appear that way, but in my experience they are more numerous than we realize. It takes time for one of the newly possessed to begin to discipline his unholy cravings, his lusts. The longer they live as host to demons, the more they can control their appetites and even command the Change to come upon them, regardless of the phases of the moon. At first, they probably don't even realize what they are, and they remember nothing of the three nights a month when their flesh reflects the monster within."

"Three nights?"

"Immediately before, the night of, and immediately after the Full Moon, Your Excellency, they change. The... sloppiness... of these Big Sur attacks suggest a newly-made werewolf. It is best to kill them before they can kill again or make others or learn to hide."

"You have leave to travel and to investigate. Call me when you can to report. Take no action without permission, Father. For the sake of the Church."

"Yes, Your Excellency."

"And do be careful," said Bishop Callahan.

"Careful has kept me alive thus far, Your Excellency. I trust in God for the rest."

CHAPTER 13:

A MURDER OF CROWS

Early Morning
Tuesday
24 May, 2016

Frank and Lela were entangled in bed when the phone rang.

"Damn," he said softly.

"Maybe we won something," she said. "A vacation to Tahiti. Cabo. Newark…"

"Maybe it's work," he said. He reached out and picked up the phone. "Yeah?"

"Is Mrs. Crow at home, please? This is Mrs. Danvers."

"Just a moment please, Mrs. Danvers," said Frank, and mouthed exaggeratedly to her as he handed her the phone. "It's your boss."

"Mrs. Danvers, good morning," said Lela.

"Good morning, Mrs. Crow. I wonder if you can be of some help to us this morning," said the older woman stiffly, as was her manner. She was a rather fussy librarian turned administrator of certain advanced years, and she had taken to treating subordinates much as she had once treated books; they were a resource to be processed and then weeded when they began to show signs of wear.

"What can I do for you?" asked Lela, who could look back into childhood and remember when Mrs. Danvers was head librarian of Monterey City Library.

"Miss Henry and Miss Grayson down at the County Library in Big Sur have both taken ill with flu, and I wonder if you would be willing to work down there for the remainder of the week. You would, of course, be compensated for travel, and I have taken the liberty of arranging for lodging in Big Sur, not far from the Library itself."

"I would be happy to help out down there," said Lela, but Frank was frowning.

"Very good, Mrs. Crow. I appreciate that I have at least one employee on whom I can thoroughly rely. Have you a pen? I shall give you the address…"

After Lela hung up with Mrs. Danvers, Frank was still frowning.

"What?" she said.

"So, you were just going to throw this old sailor over and shack up in Big Sur, eh?"

"Well, God knows it sounds restful," she said, kissing his bottom lip, "but maybe you could come with me."

"Maybe. I guess she figures you can get in on the police boat? Is that why she tapped you?"

"Well, since the road is out, I guess it's that or go on foot by the trails. There *are* advantages to being a cop's wife, right? Somewhere I was promised that. Wasn't it in the vows? Something something death do us part something something Lela gets more than suffering and worry out of her husband's damn job something something kiss the bride?"

"Yes, I remember, that was right next to richer or poorer but mostly richer blah blah boilerplate millionaire any minute…anyway I was planning on making you walk to Big Sur, maybe from here…" then his tone changed.

He said quietly, "It's a little dangerous there right now."

Then he said, "I wish you hadn't said yes."

"Well, you know Mrs. Danvers. She'd take it as a personal affront if I'd said no."

"This is true. The old lady takes it personal when people disagree with her," said Frank.

"I'm hoping to be just as cranky in my autumn years."

"Lord help us all…" he said and pulled her close. Both of their alarm clocks went off. He pulled the sheet over their heads and kissed her for a while, until she fought, twisting away from him to turn the alarms off.

She rose from the bed and on her way to the bathroom, said, "You still owe me dinner, Mr. Search and Rescue."

"I thought you owed *me* dinner, Library Lady."

"Well, I'll let you think that when you take me to the Pacific Cliffs for dinner, and then we'll retire to our intimate Big Sur casbah for the obligatory and much ballyhooed lovemaking all the rock and roll songs like to talk about."

"Just one question," he said, catching her wrist and pulling her back toward the bed.

"Shoot," she said.

"What's 'ballyhooed' mean?"

"You're the detective," she said, kissing him and scampering away. "Look it up."

While she was in the shower, Frank got a call from Detective Sergeant Ingalls.

"Frank?"

"Yeah, Sarge?"

"Someone found Abrams. Or, what's left of him."

"Where?"

"Redwood grove a half mile east of Pfeiffer. Go down there and see what you can see."

"Through that country? Someone must have put him in a car," said Frank.

"Go detect," said Ingalls. "And let's shut the door on this thing, yeah? Before anyone else gets killed.

"Right," said Frank and hung up.

Later, a Park Services SUV was waiting near Point Sur where the police boat anchored by the beach. Lela and Frank got into it, and Frank said, "Andy, you remember my wife Lela? Lela, this tall drink of water is Andy Parker, in case you'd forgotten, which is totally understandable with this guy."

"Hi, Andy. Who could forget? You danced at our wedding."

"I remember, but that's pretty impressive considering how much we all had that night," said Andy.

"Andy, can you drop Lela by the library before we head to the scene?"

"Can't see why not. It's on our way."

They dropped her off; she walked in toward the low-slung, squat library building hunkered amid the tall redwoods and then Frank said, "I'll be back soon. Don't walk alone, okay?"

"Yes, sir," she said, saluting, then she disappeared inside.

"Pretty wife," said Andy. "What's she doing with you?"

"It's for my money," said Frank.

Andy snorted.

When Lela walked in, old Hester Kinkaid was on the Circulation Desk. She was a kindly old lady whose average checkout transaction involved about seven to ten minutes of conversation on the weather, her health, her children, her grandchildren, and her great-grandchildren, her varied opinions on the various books a patron was checking out, and her deep, abiding fear and distrust of "The Google." Hester favored Lela with a smile and turned her hearing aid up.

"Lela! I haven't seen you in a month of Sundays. How are you? You know, my grandson just won the spelling bee at his school in…"

When Hester surfaced for air, some fifteen minutes later, Lela was able to get a word of greeting in and slowly edged toward the back office where she could deposit her purse and sweater.

Thus divested, she situated herself at the Reference Desk. Fortunately for her, by then Hester had found a new captive audience in a young woman checking out a book on gardening. Hester was holding forth on her strong opinions regarding the new "organic craze," and eventually, the relationship between organic foods and her bowels.

A very tall man in a dark, ankle-length duster walked in. He had close-cropped dark hair on his head and a proud red beard. He strode up to the Reference Desk, towering over Lela.

My God, she thought, *the man is seven feet if he's an inch.*

"Madame," said the man with a faint, unplaceable accent, "I wonder if you might help me with a matter of some delicacy."

"How can I help?" asked Lela.

"Well, you see," he said smiling, "I'm looking for a werewolf."

Frank and Andy bounced around inside the SUV until they came to the place where a cruiser was blocking the little dirt access road. California Highway Patrol had set up a perimeter, and they waved both men past, continuing their conversation about some arrest gone sideways. Frank and Andy strode into the shadow of an enormous ring of Redwoods, that clean smell of wood mixing with the dust and the rising heat of the day in their noses.

Several of the big trees had fallen over the years, and the Forest Service had come in and cut them at the trunks, which looked like huge flat tables. You could fit ten people around one for dinner. Abrams' boots, belt, and radio were stacked neatly on one such "table" and, not far away, blood had soaked through the top-most layers of one stump, and flies were buzzing around it in a cloud.

There was that sour smell of decay, suddenly, and the shadows seemed more menacing. Frank hadn't tossed up a meal at a crime scene for many a year, but as things began to take shape in the gloom, his stomach clenched threateningly. He heard the rasping croak of crows in the trees, the flutter of their wings. Had they been at the remains? Probably.

There was a ragged, bloody hank of mangled skin discarded nearby the bloody stump, and Frank realized someone had peeled Abrams' scalp back like the flesh of a blanched and overripe tomato.

"Who discovered this?"

"Couple of hikers this morning. We got their statements."

Frank nodded, looking around for tracks, then saw something on the stump. A neat line of pebbles. *No*, he realized, *not pebbles. Teeth.* Whoever—whatever—had taken Abrams had scalped him, removed his teeth one by one, and *eaten him* whole on this table. Slowly. Systematically. With method, intention, and practice . . .

His gut did backflips and somersaults, and he wandered back toward the SUV for a bottle of water.

"What the fuck are we dealing with, here?" he asked himself quietly, "Because animals don't do this. *Animals don't do this.*"

"A werewolf?" asked Lela, a trifle amused and trying to remain professional. She'd been at library work long enough to know you didn't mock the crazies.

"Yes, and we need to narrow down who it might be."

"We do?" she said. "How can I help you do that?"

"Well, the creature that killed those kids on Bixby Bridge, and those other two on Pfeiffer, can't be very seasoned yet—the kills are too public and too *frenzied.* I deduce he, or she" he smiled pleasantly at her, "is new at this. Probably bitten last full moon. That was April 21. So, we can check to see if someone went missing that day. Went unaccounted for. Went to hospital with a nasty bite or scratch. And who has been unaccounted for or missing these last three or four days? If a name comes up twice, perhaps we are on to something."

CHAPTER 14

THE DEATH OF RANNULF BERSKR

High summer
872 A.D.

They approached the Abbey in grim silence, hours before dawn, under cover of the English fog, and when they came to the great oaken doors, they set down the iron cage they carried as quietly as they might. The Beast-that-was-Rannulf made no sound from within, but they could smell the heavy wolfen musk, his sweat, his piss, and his hot breath steaming up like the bellows of some monstrous forge.

Three men of the advanced party began to hew the great doors with broad-bladed axes. This particular Abbey in Northern England had resisted raiders the entire summer, and that had precipitated this response from King Ragnar. They would not send fifty Vikings to burn it down. They would send Rannulf, and a party of men to pick up whatever was left of value when every last monk was dead and down the Wolf's gullet in the morning.

When the doors listed drunkenly on their great hinges, the axe men retreated, as did the box porters, back around a curve in the road and out of sight. One man remained in a white robe, standing beside the iron cage as shouts of fear rang inside the Abbey. The sound of swords singing out of sheathes and chain armor rattling in the corridors echoed crazily against the stones of the place.

So, it was true; the Christ-kneeling monks had dared to hire fighting men to defend them. The white-robed man turned and looked at the latch on the cage. He reached down slowly and whispered, "Go and kill them, Rannulf. Harm not your King's Men."

A grunt from inside the cage, then a low growl. The armored men were nearly at the doors now; they had been waiting some time for this attack, the man in white realized. He slipped the latch gently open with one long-nailed finger, then stepped back slowly and quietly, backing down the road whence they had come.

Faces and swords appeared between the hanging, splintered doors, and Rannulf exploded out of the box; a shadow made of claws and fury. The first of men-at-arms hadn't even time to scream—he landed on the tall man in the center and rode him to the ground, reaching out with his claws to the fighters immediately left and right. Rannulf's claws pressed into the eyes of the man to his right and ripped the face and faceplate of the skull away from the man on his left, while his jaws crushed helm and skull beneath of the man he had felled in his leap outward. Two other men, the last two survivors of the advanced party, hacked down with their blades across his shoulders, each on a side. Rannulf roared at the bite of the swords, then slashed upward, not cutting into the chainmail with his claws, but rather lifting both men and hurling them into the stonework of the ceiling with bone-crushing force. They both fell heavily and at sickening angles: a pair of broken marionettes. Rannulf padded on, farther into the Abbey sniffing quietly with a hunter's patience, the wounds on his back blackening and scabbing over, then disappearing.

He smelled them before he heard them. Their sour fear-stink spreading like a low cloud out from under the doorways of the dining hall. He slunk quietly to the door and listened to them whisper their prayers, listened to their hearts pound inside their twig-thin rib-cages. His mouth began to water. The monks had been kind enough to congregate in one place with one exit. Thirty or forty of them. He stepped back some distance then charged the door and leaped for it, shattering it into kindling as he hurtled into the darkened, torchlit hall.

They moaned and wailed and cried out in blind, animal terror. He smelled fresh piss as he rushed forward to meet them. They huddled, trembling like so many sheep before him, but a tall man in lamellar armor and a broad round shield interposed himself, screaming fury and defiance.

Rannulf bounced off the man's shield, gained his feet and came low, snapping for the man's ankle-bones. The man brought down his silver-handled spatha with a sweeping blow to Rannulf's jaws and split his lip, nearly shearing the top of his snout off—Rannulf recoiled, howling and gurgling in pain.

The tall warrior advanced, body-checked Rannulf with his round shield, catching him snout first, and sent him reeling against the stone wall of the chamber, just beneath a torch sconce. Rannulf roared in rage, his wound already beginning to knit. The tall man knocked the torch down with a light gesture of his blade, showering the wolf's eyes in sparking coals, burning his flesh so he snapped impotently at the flames, distracted momentarily as the man wound up and impaled Rannulf's chest, burying his blade silver hilt-deep and pinning him to the flagstones of the hall.

Rannulf had no breath, but simply reached out for the warrior in blind panic, catching his sword arm and crushing his wrists, scratching madly with his rear paws and knocking away the tall man's shield. Rannulf caught a breath and gurgled, scratching and slamming the tall man this way and that, biting at his shoulders and crushing his arms, scratching at his face, his bowels, his legs, ripping pieces of knitted iron away from the lamellar and sending them spinning into the dark as he shuddered and scratched and bit convulsively, then more slowly, then finally he took the man by the neck and hurled him away as with a child's toy; the knight fell hard, limp and barely breathing.

Then Rannulf growled and whimpered mournfully, and before the eyes of those thirty monks he meant to massacre, he shuddered and died. His body began to change, to diminish, his hair fell out in clumps, and soon he was nothing but a bloody North Man, pale and red-haired. And dead.

So passed Rannulf, son of Olav, son of Og, Berserker of King Ragnar, who died in battle and passed on his curse to the warrior who killed him; the first of many in a long line carrying his curse.

CHAPTER 15:
ADDITIONS AND SUBTRACTIONS

Noon
Tuesday
24 May, 2016

"The way I see it," said Frank, riding back with Andy after the forensics team had taken over the crime scene, "we have two different MOs here. One seems like an almost rabid animal; this thing rips car doors open and feasts in the middle of a major highway. It kills on roadways and public beaches. It's savage and furious and *very* messy."

"Yeah, okay, and the other?"

"This new crime scene isn't like that. This other suspect disappeared an armed man with no witnesses, nobody reports screams, no blood, no signs of a struggle, nothing... brought him out to this prepared place undetected, and slowly, methodically fed on him, leaving almost nothing behind but a peeled back scalp and a few surgically-removed teeth. It's almost the difference between a young man's exuberance and an old man's practiced hand."

"Like that joke," said Andy.

"What joke is that?" asked Frank, and then, "Mind if I smoke?"

"Hell, yes, I mind. This is a California State Vehicle, buddy. They'll put my balls in a vice, and besides, those things'll kill you."

Frank sighed.

"Anyway," Andy said. "The joke. You know. Old bull and a young bull are sitting up on a hill looking over the herd. Young Bull says, 'Let's run down there and *fuck us a cow*.' Old Bull looks at him, shakes his head, 'Let's *walk* down and fuck 'em all.'"

Frank chuckled, nodded. They were silent a moment, then Andy said, "So, maybe these are two... animals? Very smart animals? They're surely not men."

"I seem to remember Lela brought home a book once called *The Man-Eaters of Tsavo* about a pair of lions who very successfully preyed on dozens of men in Africa for a while. They were smart enough to elude hunters, escape traps, slip through defenses, and they didn't kill like normal lions. When they finally got caught, it turned out they were diseased, and really big, even for male lions."

"You think they're lions? Escaped from someone's exotic pet collection?" said Andy.

"Well, but even really sick lions wouldn't carry a man half a mile or more and *eat him whole at a table*, much less remove his teeth and hair. And they don't have opposable thumbs."

"Some kind of ape?"

"...it doesn't add up. None of this adds up," said Frank. "The older one has done this before. No doubt about it. And maybe that's one of his spots. Forensics will find evidence of older kills, if there are any to find."

They pulled up to the library at around one in the afternoon, and Lela was sitting at a bench outside the main doors, presumably on her break, talking to an enormous bald man with a bushy, red beard in a huge black duster. They both had paper cups of coffee and seemed to be talking amiably.

She waved them over smiling, "Hi Andy, hi Frank. This is Nob. Nob and I have been talking about werewolves..."

Billy walked back the long miles to the Fernwood Tavern, where he presumed he had left his Caddie. It was there, a light coat of dust from air-drying by the side of the road after the rains and the morning mists, but it was whole and waiting. He breathed relief, then patted the hood and strode into the tavern.

The bartender, Aria, pretty, lithe and tattooed with rather more eye makeup than she needed, half smiled at him then frowned, "Hey, Billy. You okay?" she asked.

"Yeah," he said. "Why wouldn't I be?"

"They were talking about getting your car towed if you didn't come back soon. Where they'd tow it, I don't know, what with the One being out and all."

"One? Highway One?"

"Yeah, where have you been? Big landslide on the cliffs Saturday, north and south. We're getting supplies in by ferry, but we're pretty well cut off. They're saying summer is shot, and a lot of businesses are going to fold."

"I, um... have been writing. Just, lost track of the world, I guess," he said, but he wasn't a good liar, and she didn't look convinced.

"You know how it is. Hashtag writing life," he said a bit lamely.

"Right," she said, glancing at the clock. It said *12:01pm*. "It's after noon. Get you a drink?"

"If I say no, I think they take away my writer's card," he said. "How about pale ale?"

"Sierra okay?"

"Sure," he said.

She pulled him a pint and laid it on the bar, and he sat. There was no one else there at that hour. In truth, Big Sur was nowhere near as busy at it normally was—traffic on the highway was almost nonexistent, and there were no tourists of any variety. Aria was not alone in feeling it was spooky.

"...roads went out on Saturday?" he said quietly, "Uh... hey, Aria? What day is it?"

She fixed him with a look between pity and concern, "It's Tuesday," she said. "Did you hit your head?"

"I'm not sure," he said. "I can't remember anything after leaving the bar on Friday."

"You didn't drink much, but you seemed a little antsy when you left."

He tried for an image of Friday night, but it was as blank as a white sheet of paper fresh before he fed it into his typewriter. Nothing. Total blackout. White out. Whatever. Billy shook his head in frustration.

"Weird," he said, finally, and sipped his beer. Then, because it tasted good and he was powerfully thirsty, he downed it.

"Another?" she asked.

"Sure," he said.

She poured. He drank and noticed something curious reaching for his second glass... his fingernails had grown since Friday. Half an inch in three days? And the nails themselves looked *thicker* somehow. Less transparent. Darker. He thought of the blood on his hands when he woke up and downed the second beer.

"Slow down, cowboy," she said. "Or you're going to have to walk home again," she said.

"Actually," he said with dawning surprise, "I'm... fine." Two beers that fast and he didn't have any pleasant tingle in his legs or warmth spreading through his stomach. He was as sober as a Baptist funeral.

"Heard that before," she said with a soft smile. Was she flirting with him, suddenly?

He realized she was. A change had come over her. Some kind of heat passed between them. Something almost animal in its attraction. He wanted to climb over the bar and sniff up her leg, rip her panties off with his teeth... she was leaning in against the bar, giving him a better view of the soft crush of her breasts. It hadn't been like this before between them, had it? He felt himself growing hard, felt himself beginning to move toward her, then stopped. No.

Something asked him why not? Deep inside, without words. *Why not?*

"I've got to get going," he said, and reached for a wallet that wasn't there. Where was his wallet? Where were his clothes from the night before? Where, he asked himself with mounting alarm, were his keys? "I, uh, forgot my wallet and my keys, I can… uh... pay you back later."

"I can drive you back to your place to find them," she said, a slight smile playing at her lips. "It's almost my lunch break."

Why not?

"Sure," he said, his spine electric with a sudden flare of sex. "Why not?"

CHAPTER 16

LANVAL RISING

"He who fights monster should beware, lest he become a monster himself" –Friedrich Nietzsche
High summer
872 A.D.
Northern England

Lanval, the Frankish Knight who had killed the Vikings' wolfwere, had been carried to some monk's cell and laid on a rope bed. They expected him to be dead in hours, or less. Rannulf had crushed his arms at the wrists, pulled them out of joint at the shoulders, and flayed his skin to ribbons from chest and shoulders down to split-open fingers. The death throes of the beast had been fearsome to behold, but unimaginably painful to endure.

Lanval himself felt like one enormous pulsing wound. They had brought hot water and patched his wounds with clean linens, now beginning to soak through with scarlet. He drifted in and out of consciousness. He heard the monks whispering that he would be dead by dawn and praying for his soul and singing their Aves that they had been spared. Apparently, the North Men had fled when their wolf had not returned. Probably they would be back soon with a more conventional force to kill them all. Lanval gripped his sword like a man drowning holds to a line thrown from shore.

He shivered and trembled and sweat, and inside it felt as if his very bones were baking in the village bread oven.

"...Maman! Don't… don't... don't p-put me in the o-o-oven. Mon *Dieu*…" It was too painful to thrash, or to move, or to think, or to cry out. Faces came out of the shadows. The faces of wolves and monsters and demons of the pit who wore the faces of men while wolf faces lurked beneath their mummer's masks.

The Abbot, a greying man of perhaps fifty winters, entered the cell at dawn and performed the Last Rites. He whispered thanks and other words that Lanval could not retain or even properly understand.

Lanval dreamed.

He was at table in a dark and empty hall, seated at the far side of an enormous table with a King whose beetle-black eyes filled him with low, nauseating fear. The King's hair was long and very dark, nearly bristling like that of a beast... in fact, his expression seemed not to change, as if he wore a human face as a mask and his true face beneath. Something told Lanval that that when that face was revealed, it would drive him howling into madness.

"Eat," the King had said, and Lanval regarded the sumptuous feast at the table and realized his own ravenous, bottomless hunger.

He reached for the golden loaf of crisp bread, the smooth yellow cream of the butter, the delicately spiced roast chicken, a fat wedge of gently-yielding cheese, the jeweled promise of crisp autumn apples, and the cool delight of snow-chilled ale, and the pleasant zest of hot mulled wine; he ate and drank, drank and ate, and still he could not fill his belly; the more he had, the more he wanted, with a deep, abiding, relentless lust.

The smells were sharp and tantalizing in his nose and on his tongue. Lanval ate until his eyes filled up with darkness, until the ale and the bread and the wine and the roast and the apples had but one taste, and that taste was the hot coppery cloying red salt of blood. He looked up, and the King's face was the Wolf's face, The Wolf of All Wolves, the Great Wolf of the North, the Wolf Who Would Devour the Aesir at Ragnarok, Fenrir Himself, impossibly huge as mountains and storms and great waves on the sea are huge.

Yet, it sat somehow at this great table and said, "Eat."

But before him was a table of gore and goblets of bile, high stacked plates of intestine and marrowbones and baskets of ears and fingers and noses and toes, and stuffed in the center was Lanval himself, flayed open and unblinking and naked in the firelight like a roasted pig.

"Eat," said Fenrir, his voice the growl of colliding mountains. "Eat."

Lanval opened his mouth to scream but could make no sound. His gorge was rising. He wanted to vomit, but rather . . . he began to howl.

When he awoke, the pain was gone. His wounds were gone beneath his bandages.

He somehow knew.

The twitter of birds outside was as loud as war drums, and the light streaming in from the windows was blinding. The hallway was slick with blood... and littered with the bodies of monks. Beneath him, the Abbot's face was fixed in a look of abject terror, and a gaping, ragged hole was congealing with stilled blood where his throat should have been. Lanval slid off the older man, tasting the blood in his mouth, looking down at the flesh under his fingernails, tasting the fleshy pulp still hot in his mouth. *Eat.*

There was no one for miles around to hear his screams.

CHAPTER 17:

COMES A HUNTER

Tuesday Afternoon
May 24, 2016

The priest hiked into Big Sur over the trails and then along the now all-but-defunct Highway One, Army surplus rucksack slung over his back. He wore a navy blue flannel button-down shirt and canvas olive drab cargo pants cinched with a leather web belt.

In his bag were sundries: a First-Aid kit, fresh clothes, a rifle broken down for travel, and three boxes of special, custom-made ammunition. In a holster, concealed in his belt holster and under his shirt, was a Glock 43 loaded with seven silver-jacketed hollow point rounds.

Father Giovanni had spent the evening before, very carefully, very methodically filling the tiny bowl of each bullet with half a dropper-full of cyanide, then dripping exactly three drops of thick red sealing wax over the top of each one. He etched a cross into each of them, and when he had finished, he blessed the stacked boxes of bullets, whispering the words, "*In name of the Father, and of the Son, and of the Holy Ghost. O glorious Archangel St. Michael, Prince of the heavenly host, defend us in battle, and in the struggle, which is ours against the principalities and Powers, against the rulers of this world of darkness, against spirits of evil in high places.*"

And Tuesday afternoon he had followed the road into town to find, and kill, the werewolf he knew must be here.

Dry and dusty, Father Giovanni walked into the main dining room of The Big Sur River Inn. He shrugged off his pack and sat at a corner table where he could watch the room and the doors and the large windows that looked outside. He looked around with eyes that held the details of everything he saw.

It was always this way on a hunt, he mused. One of the... thrills? It wasn't the wrong word. One of the thrills of hunting these particular beasts was that they might be anyone. The fresh-faced young hostess who seated him might be disposed to devour a man when the moon rises full over the land. The young hiker at the bar. The old man eating quietly at an adjacent table. It could be anyone. It sharpened his senses, as always. But there were ways to tell.

They were usually alone. The experienced ones, *far more dangerous* in the priest's experience than the newly infected, generally knew that to involve others meant death for those others, sooner or later. While werewolves young in their Moons had unbridled, animal savagery that made them sloppy, it also meant they usually woke up naked in compromising (often bloody and murderous) situations. As such, days after the Change, they were usually frightened, disoriented, and confused. More experienced wolves remembered more and might, in certain cases, be able to summon and control the change, steer the rage and hunger, and anticipate situations of danger. They were difficult prey but their preparation sometimes gave them away.

People who disappeared at dusk three days a month and who had to either travel far or restrain themselves someplace secluded in order not to kill, or not to kill locally, were traceable. They might be able to shift at other times, in moments of extremis: in rage, or pain, or during sleep, but all werewolves had to change by moonrise (sometimes dusk, but moonrise *at the latest*) on the night before, the night of, and the night after the Full Moon. They tended to change back to a human shape by dawn, but this could vary.

He had known wolves who never slipped the wolf skin once in those 72 hours, but no amount of research seemed to find a predictable, repeatable pattern to this. Likewise, sometimes the infection was mercurial. Some who were bitten or clawed did not change, and others might change if they kissed or had sexual contact with one of the infected immediately before, during, or after a change. Such things did happen. Father Giovanni shuddered at the memory of his last hunt. A waiter came, and the priest ordered a Tri-Tip sandwich, then thanked the young man.

It had been bad, that last time. A pack had grown to a dozen in a small hamlet in Washington State, not far from the Oregon line. They were led by a clever Alpha (usually the eldest and strongest wolf, often the one who had infected the others) who had prepared against hunters. The local sheriff and several deputies watched the roads in and out of town and pulled over anyone they didn't recognize. They'd sniff gun oil right off and then mark where the hunter stayed. The others embedded in town would watch, wait, mark what questions the newcomer asked.

This was how Father Bennet met his end.

Father Giovanni had taken a different approach. He was not inclined to put his head into a noose. Instead, he waited for one of the deputies he was certain of: the one who looked up, wincing at the sound of the dog whistle. The deputy caught Father Giovanni's bullet right between the eyes on a stretch of highway between the Interstate and town, far away from all his wolfen kin.

Then, Father Giovanni had taken the police car, sunk it in the river and hung the dead man from a high branch outside the old logging cabin where he would make his stand. The wolves, he reckoned, wouldn't find the corpse via scent until the change was on them that night. Their higher reason would be dormant— they wouldn't realize they'd been bottlenecked by two streams in the small box canyon. And from high on the lip of that canyon, he could take with his rifle the ones who didn't die from his daisy chain of six improvised silver, homemade Composition B Claymore Mines.

The young River Inn waiter brought the priest his sandwich. Father Giovanni thanked him, his eyes sliding over the young man's fingernails. The infected had fingernails that grew very quickly and were often more opaque than most. Recent cutting was suspicious, as were unusually long nails; painted nails of extraordinary length were suspicious, too. The young man had none of these signs.

"Thank you," said Father Giovanni. "What's your name?"

"I'm Cameron," said the waiter. "Let me know if there's anything I can get for you."

"Cameron, it's rather quiet in here," looking around at the dozen or so people dining inside and out. "Is it usually like this?"

"No, we're usually much busier, but since the highway went out it's been less traffic."

"Yes, I can imagine," said Father Giovanni. "I suppose you live locally. A commute would be challenging."

"Yes, I'm local," he said.

"I wonder, do you know much about what I've read in the paper regarding some animal attacks here recently? I find locals always know more than reporters," he said with a soft smile, as if they were sharing a confidence.

"Just that something attacked a couple on Bixby Bridge and maybe out by Pfeiffer Beach, and that they're saying be careful about going out after dark. Might be a rabid bear or something."

Giovanni nodded, "I see. Very good advice. I hope they catch it soon."

Cameron nodded amiably in agreement and moved off. The priest began to eat his sandwich. On the hunt, he thought, food tastes better.

The box canyon had been an excellent killing ground, and he had taken nine with the claymores, and two with the rifle afterwards, but the Alpha had been clever and sent his troops before him, then moved to flank Father Giovanni in the tree line when he broke from cover. It had been a big beast, but silent as a moth's wings brushing silk. Giovanni, no fool, had not moved from his place of concealment on the hill for fifteen minutes, waiting, listening, and counting what was left of the bodies over and over, coming up always with 11 dead. Of 12. Where was the last one?

He waited. Waited. Heard nothing and wondered if he had been deafened by the improvised Claymores—there was a steady ringing in his ears. Finally, he broke from concealment and very slowly stalked down the lip of the canyon toward the smoldering ruin of the cabin below—there hadn't been much fire or much smoke—the little structure had been essentially blown apart by the shockwaves of each blast, timed a second apart. Nevertheless, bits and boards still smoked with tiny fires here and there.

The only reason he heard the twig break behind him was because he'd been waiting for it, and as he turned and levelled his rifle, the beast was already in the air above him; falling darkness before the moon.

Giovanni had fired three times in quick succession, and the beast landed on him, jaws champing and slathering. It was all he could do; he rolled off the edge of the cliffside, grasping at what he might to slow his descent. He caught a knobbled pine root ten feet down and clutched it, letting the rifle fall to the forest floor forty feet below. His arm nearly wrenched out of socket, tearing a ragged scream from his throat, but his grip held. Above him, churned up slate, tiny rocks, and dirt fell off the edges of the cliff and down into his eyes and onto his shoulders as the werewolf above clawed and roared its final seconds of life. When it was silent, he began slowly and carefully to climb, the pain in his shoulder excruciating. When he breasted the top of the cliff, the wolf's muzzle and jaws met his eyes, and it growled...

...then snapped…

...then closed its eyes and began to melt away into an old woman's face.

Giovanni breathed relief at the memory, even as he sat at the Big Sur River Restaurant and felt the phantom soreness in his shoulder flair. Afterward, he had drawn his sidearm and put two silver-jacketed hollow points in each of the dead werewolves that still had heads, despite the fact they had all reverted to human skin—a sure sign of death. He was a careful and deliberate man, after all, he thought to himself, then regarded his screaming shoulder. All evidence to the contrary, said a wry inner voice. Had the Alpha landed on him, scratched, bitten, he might have been infected. This power of infection was true of any werewolf, of course. He would have killed it and then he would have killed himself. But it didn't happen. Not that time.

Of course, this was a problem that werewolf hunters, vampire hunters, demon hunters who worked for the Order of the Sword of God all wrestled with. Suicide, the Church taught, is a mortal sin. To a one, though, in training and out of it, Father Giovanni had never met a single *Gladius Dei* hunter who was willing to become what he (or she) hunted.

Not one.

They were all universally committed to death first. It was an unspoken tenet of their Holy Crusade. Damnation before dishonor.

Cameron brought the check, and Father Giovanni thanked him. "I wonder if there is vacancy at this Inn? I should like to stay for some time."

"Yes, sir. The front desk is just around the corner, and they can get you taken care of."

"Very good. Thank you. By the way, Cameron," said the priest, thumbing bills in his wallet to lay down as a tip, "I wonder if you'd do me a favor and let me know if you hear more about these attacks. I'm—" here he laid down forty dollars on the table, "very interested."

Cameron tried to smile without smiling too much, "Uh, yes sir. No problem. Thank you, sir."

"Call me Giovanni," he said with a smile, and they shook hands, "I'll see you tomorrow for lunch."

After he secured a room (quaint, comfortable, rustic, with a view of the river, which was more like a creek beneath the trees here), Father Giovanni sat on the bed and assembled his rifle. He loaded it with its custom silver ammunition and made a phone call from the room.

"I'm here, Your Excellency," he said into the receiver, "and I am beginning."

CHAPTER 18:
BILLY AND ARIA MAKE MISTAKES

Tuesday Afternoon
May 24, 2016

The fucking had been good. Aria and Billy agreed on that without having to speak. Normally fairly uninhibited anyway, Aria had surprised herself at her wanton abandon, her unreasonable desire to consume him, like his flesh was some kind of drug, the heat of his scent some intoxicant gone to her head or directly to her loins.

It surprised Billy, too. He had always been good-looking and had never wanted for female company, but she was almost animal in a way that, at times nearly frightened him. She had collapsed, exhausted, on his (he had learned, rather noisy) bed, and they caught their breaths, dozed in and out lightly, his arms around her as she faced away toward the mirror on the closet door.

He fell into a dream. He was running through a forest, claws instead of hands, fur instead of flesh, racing effortlessly. Scents like sirens over the sound of traffic in a metropolis, competing and overlapping. Rabbit. Heat. Fear. Scrambling. Loose dirt. Deer piss, a doe in estrus, blood, now, zinging and electric like a tongue on a high voltage socket, frying and shorting and cooking his cortex with its scent *bloodbloodbloodbloodblood* like the pulse in his ears and the growl in his belly and the roll of his shoulders and flanks as he covered the distance over the forest floor to the sweetest and darkest and most primordial of all scents: *blood*.

In his dream, Billy, or the wolf that had Billy asleep inside it, was drawing to a clearing of redwoods where the blood scent was nearly a visible crimson wave. Something was in there. He moved cautiously, slowly, hackles rising, fear bubbling beside the blood frenzy in his belly, the erection he hadn't registered was flagging suddenly… there were wet snaps and pops and cracks of what he simply *knew* was bone. He peered through the foliage, and there sat an enormous wolf as black as the bottom of the sea, its head monstrous, eyes lolling as it ate, systematically and with great relish, on the flat stump of a great fallen redwood tree. It was eating a man, but not as a wolf would eat, rather as a man eats at a feast. Slowly. Savoringly. It looked over at him and growled low in its throat. "*Eat.*"

Billy awoke and looked up, gasping and in a cold sweat. Aria wore the black wolf's face in the mirror. He screamed, and she growled, lunging for his throat.

Billy awoke and looked up, gasping and in a cold sweat. Aria was gone. The shower was running. He didn't want to look in the mirror, but when he did only his own frightened eyes looked back at him in the same face he always woke up to.

The water stopped, and she called to him, "Do you have a fresh towel? The one hanging up smells like a man."

He went to the linen closet and then to the bathroom, handing her the fresh towel. She smiled at his nakedness in her nakedness. It wasn't an invitation, exactly, but rather unabashed nakedness after something much more unabashed had passed between them.

"If you'd been pouring and I'd been drinking, I'd wonder what you put in my drink, handsome," she said.

"Whatever it was, it was good stuff," he said.

"Right," she said, toweling off, "but I'd better get back to Fernwood before they can me."

"Or you could stay, and we could do it again," he said with a smile.

"Sure," she said. "But I need to eat." And yet, she was already moving toward him, the towel slipping to the bathroom floor. A hunger in her eyes.

What was happening? She had every intention to leave. Why had they come? Keys? Wallet? Yes... did he... find those? She was kissing him. She was in his arms. There was something animal about him, she decided as she let him into her again, just before conscious thought switched off.

When they surfaced for air, hours later, she called in and explained she'd become violently ill. The boss was understanding, as she'd never missed a day before. That caught in her mind.

She was extremely responsible. She'd never done anything like this in her life. Sex with a stranger when she was supposed to be at work? Ready to leave and then weak-kneed at the very suggestion of Round 2?? Aria wasn't that girl. She was in grad school at Sarah Lawrence, summering back home and working to make extra bread, crashing with friends so she didn't cramp her parents. How was she back in Billy's bed at dusk, memorizing the lines of his face with her fingertips and breathing in his scent like it was dark chocolate crack?

"What's going on here?" she asked, poking his chest gently, "Do you always have this effect on the ladies?"

"Just Big Sur ladies with tattoos who work at Fernwood and pour tasty beer, so far," he said. "Wait, are you a Big Sur lady?"

"Yes, I'm local. Grew up here. Parents grew up here. Their parents moved to Monterey County from San Francisco in the 30s. What about you? Where are you from?"

"I'm from Coulterville, originally. Little town in the hills near Yosemite. Went to college at Iowa State on a writing scholarship. Published a book. Working to churn out a novel while I'm here over summer, then maybe back home. I don't know. Maybe not."

"Why don't you know?" she asked, tracing the curves of his shoulders in the half-light with her fingers.

"There was—I had something happen up there last month. Bad. I couldn't stay after. Couldn't write. Couldn't sleep. Couldn't breathe. So, threw it all in the Caddie and drove south until I got here. It felt like the right place to stop."

"What kind of accident?" she asked.

His jaw tightened and there was a long pause, "It's hard to talk about."

She could feel him trembling under her hands, and she pulled him close. "It's okay. You don't have to talk about it."

He nodded against her.

"Thanks," he said, but he feared that he would talk about it, and when he did, he might start screaming, and if he started screaming, he might not ever stop. He studiously avoided the mirror on the closet and was grateful when it was too dark to see it at all.

CHAPTER 19:

DISCOVERIES

Tuesday Afternoon
24 May, 2016

Frank and Lela and Nob and Andy sat down on the benches outside the library.

"Werewolves?" said Frank.

Nob shrugged. "Well. Let me explain. My name is Nob, I own *The Cauldron* and—"

Andy snorted, "Isn't that a mysticism and hokum shop? Sell voodoo dolls to tourists. Now what're you selling?"

Nob narrowed his eyes at Andy. His physical presence was imposing, but his eyes were suddenly less friendly and that was weirdly worse. Andy shifted uncomfortably.

"There are things in this world most people can't explain or don't care to know. Can you explain what you have seen?"

"Where are you from, sir?" asked Frank, drawing a cigarette and a dark look from Lela. He put the cigarette away with the ghost of a sigh.

"Nob. Call me Nob. I was born in Norway."

"Hence the accent," said Frank.

Yes,"

"And how long have you been here?"

"I bought the shop fifteen years ago."

"The thing that did this was very tall and very strong and walked on two legs. How tall are you, Mr. Nob?" asked Frank.

"I'm seven feet. But I'm not the one you're looking for. I can help you find it, though. We have a little time, now, unless I'm mistaken."

"Because the moon is waning?"

"Yes," said Nob, "and if we can figure out who was missing over the weekend and who resurfaced Monday or today…"

"I thought werewolves only changed on the night of the full moon," said Andy.

Nob looked at him again but with kinder eyes, "The books I've read say they can change at will, once they learn the trick, but they all change the night before a full moon, the night when the moon is at the full, and the night after that. Three nights. That means there will have been at least three attacks, although sometimes there are multiples in a night. My guess is this one is young. Older ones can guide the Change, and the Hunger, and they avoid eating people on public highways.

They find the sort that won't be missed, out in places no one will know what happened."

"You mean, werewolves eat people three days a month, and no one has caught on yet?" asked Frank.

"You know, 750,000 people go missing in the U.S. alone every year," said Lela. They all looked at her, a bit startled. "Most of them just leave without telling anyone and turn up in some other state far away years later. Some are kidnapped. Some just . . . vanish."

"You're saying the werewolves get them?" asked Frank, reaching for a cigarette, deciding against it, and setting his jaw in frustration.

"I don't know," said Lela. "Maybe not. But it's sort of like what they say about people who drown or go missing at sea. They call it drowning, because they can't know what really happened. Maybe they got a cramp and drowned, and no one saw, and no one recovered the body. Or maybe a shark swam up. A big one, from the depths, came up and ate some poor soul, brains, balls, boots and all, but no one saw, so no one knows, and the sharks aren't telling. The people who keep records call it drowning."

Frank shivered, and then something moved in the corner of his vision, and he turned his head, then grew very still. The power lines running the length of the road were black and nearly bowed with what was easily a thousand black crows, almost perfectly still and staring at the people seated on the benches. Frank looked left, right, fore, aft, and saw thousands upon thousands of glittering black eyes gleaming out at him from the shadows of limbs and eaves and rooftops and boughs.

Lela gasped, Andy breathed, "What the fuck?" and Nob sighed. "They're nothing to worry about," he said. "They're on our side. Sort of."

"Let's go inside," said Lela, "They're giving me the creeps."

They did.

Inside the little library, Frank asked Nob (now in his stage-whisper library voice) "What do you mean they're on our side?"

"They warned me of the *varulv* to begin with," said Nob, quietly. Lela found them a quiet table near the rear of a set of book stacks.

Frank felt as if he were dealing with a crazy, but Nob didn't seem exactly crazy, and those crows were still looking at him in his mind's eye.

"Why? And how do they know?" asked Frank.

"You know crows are incredibly intelligent birds, right? I mean, they use tools, teach each other tricks, use distinctive language patterns that experts say may be their names for each other, and they recognize human faces," said Lela.

Frank's mouth hung open a moment before he shut it, "No. I didn't know that. But even if they're wicked smart, how do they know about werewolves?"

"Why would a carrion bird and a thousand of his closest friends not know about a predator leaving stuff around for them?" asked Lela.

"And why would they tell us? Or tell Nob?" asked Andy quietly.

"Because I'm a Gothi of the Old Religion, and we have an agreement," said Nob quietly, "an agreement that goes back a long way. They were priests of the Aesir, the old gods of the North Men before Christianity came."

"You and the birds have an agreement?" asked Frank, almost compulsively drawn to his pack of cigarettes now.

"The gods sent the birds. Or one god did."

"Oh. Gods and werewolves and crows who honor agreements. Well, I'll look into it," said Frank. "Thanks for your time, Mr. Nob."

"Just Nob," said Nob.

"You don't have a last name?"

"I do, it's Nob Haraldson, but you can just call me Nob. I wouldn't put any of this in a report. I realize it sounds crazy, but you should realize it's true. Consider what you have seen: A beast of strength most bears can't boast, that doesn't hunt like an animal, but that has an animal's claws and teeth. A creature with opposable thumbs, who attacks not one person alone, but two at a time or more. A creature who is savage and methodical by turns. A creature that can make a man disappear from one place."

"With all due respect, Mr. Nob, I think there's an animal. Maybe a sick animal. And possibly some kind of cult or cannibal ring that's unleashing it. And maybe they've got that Old Time religion. And maybe they have a 'Gothi' cultivating this idea. I don't believe in werewolves, although I consider myself an open-minded guy. I do believe in people with crazy ideas doing terrible things, though. And that's from experience."

"You're the detective, Detective," said Nob. "But I'll be here when the facts lead you to one inevitable conclusion. Because it is the truth."

"Thanks for your time," said Frank, rising to leave, and Andy rose with him. Frank looked at Lela, "I'll pick you up at closing time, yeah?"

"Sounds good," she said, smiling, and as the Ranger and the Detective walked away, she said quietly to Nob, "It's been a pleasure meeting you, Nob."

Nob rose and took her small hand in his huge one.

"The pleasure was mine, ma'am. I hope we meet again."

"Call me Lela," she said.

"Lela, then," he said. "Thank you for listening. I wonder if you'll give me a call if you hear of anyone who disappeared over the weekend."

"Sure," she said.

"Thank you," he said, with curious solemnity.

As he left, Lela got the sense that he knew more, much more, than he had said, although what he had said threw science, rationality, and empiricism into a cocked hat. Was he the leader of some cannibal cult? Lela didn't think so. She was a good judge of character, and Nob was a gentle soul, at bottom. She was certain of it. But she was equally certain there was more in his mind than he had said. Much more.

Nob went outside and wandered over to a nearby tree, looking up at the still nearly motionless crows.

"Show me who did the murders at Bixby Creek Bridge. Show me this *varulv*."

The crows, as one bird, took flight from the trees amid a din of ragged caws and pounding black wings, feathers swirling. They flocked in a great spiral rising in the sky. Then they turned south and began to fly as a black cloud toward Billy Hatfield's cabin.

CHAPTER 20

THE THING ON THE MOORS

North York Moors
Spring, 1197 A.D.

It was said among the peasants that people disappeared on the Black Moor. They whispered that there
were beasts there that roamed the mist, monsters
who wore human faces until the rising of the moon.
They spoke of an old man who lived on the edge of the
moor, who called himself Lanval. He was, they said,
mad to live so close to that awful place and mad to live
so far from town at his age. He had lived there, already
a very old man, when the grandfathers and grandmoth-
ers of the village of Whitby were small children. He had
been a farmer and kept pigs for many years but had no
wife, no children, and it seemed that the deep furrows
and crags of his face and the knobbled curl of his ancient

hands grew ever more deep and cragged and knobbled year by year.

And yet, he would come into the village once every fortnight to sell a pig at market or to buy sundries. Ever there was gossip that he was dead and did not know it, or that he would be dead soon by the things on the moor, or that he had made a deal with the Devil and so would not die. They called him "Methuselah" behind his back, and indeed if the old fellow from the Bible had met Lanval, they might have been in sympathy for one another.

He walked very slowly and deliberately, slightly hunched over, favoring his right leg. The whispers preceded his coming and closed behind him like a curtain of gossip as he went. They said he'd had a wife once, but that he had killed her and her lover and sunk them in a bog. They said he'd been cursed by a witch. They said he'd been a knight cast out by the king for consorting with evil spirits. They bruited about every manner of outré horror about the old man, for he was strange, and he was solitary, and he was very, very old.

One sodden April morning, he came into the village to sell a pig, but after the transaction Old Lanval left his coin purse on a post outside Colm Marsten's pig pens. Marsten didn't notice until afternoon, and he stared a long time at the coin purse. Part of him, the better part, told him the old man was poor, whatever stories the women around the fires told each other about his secret gold hoard. He should return the coin purse. It was only right. Another voice, a softer voice, said he should only *inventory* the coin purse. Just to make sure. Just in case anything should happen. Yes. Just in case. Better to know how much he would *owe* Lanval, should the purse fall down a well, or be swept away by a river.

Marsten had walked by the post where Lanval left his coin purse half a dozen times since he discovered it, eye straying as he went from field to pen, pen to field, back to the pen again. Finally, he snatched it up and weighed it in his hands. It felt pleasantly full. Well, it would do no harm to count it, after all. He walked into the dark little woodshed and poured the contents on the bare boards of the belly-high counter. He counted, and sweat formed on his upper lip and his brow. They could never tax what they did not know about, he thought. And this could set them up nicely if there should be a bad winter or two. He heard the rain began to patter, then pound on the thatched roof of the woodshed.

"He'll be back for it. He'll remember where he left it," said Marsten, his voice startling him in the dark, "I'll—I'll have to return it," he said, scooping up the pounds and returning them to the money purse. But a darker voice whispered to him, "*Perhaps. Perhaps. But perhaps that old man will forget. Yes, perhaps as old as he is, he will not remember, and it is easy to say you found nothing.*"

Marsten considered this, the pleasant weight of ten years' wages in his hand. *No, he'll remember. He'll come back. He'll accuse me, and they'll hang me for a thief,* Marsten thought.

It was ten miles from the village to Lanval's cottage, and it was already afternoon, but Marsten set off, telling himself he was an honest man returning lost property. He hurried as quickly as he might, his belly hot with strange, nameless fear. At every bend in the road, he looked to see the old man hobbling toward home, but the rutted roads were empty, the rain began to drive in earnest, and Marsten continued the weary miles onward as the grey light began to fail.

The stories of the old women came back to him now. The horrors on the moor after dark rose like a fog in his imagination. He considered turning back, keeping the coin purse, burying it, but it felt more like a curse and a menace the old man had left deliberately to bedevil and confuse him. As he trotted on, his conviction grew stronger that Lanval had done this to him deliberately for some nefarious purpose, although the old man had always seemed kindly and harmless to him, no matter what they whispered of him in the village.

On he walked in the rain, his traveling cloak draped over him against the wet, hood pulled over his head. Then he heard something behind him. At first, he thought it was nothing, but then it came again. A cry of some kind. He turned and saw nothing through the thick rain and rising mist. He resumed his walk. What would his Morag say of him when he came home dripping wet late tonight? What would that redheaded harridan say when he told her he had given back a fortune? She was always something of a skinflint, and without a doubt she would harangue him mightily for his choice to hurry away into the rain to return the old man's purse,

much less to return it at all when it could have fur-
nished her with comforts they would never otherwise
possess. He could almost hear her shrill pronounce-
ments on his feeble-minded pig-farmer's uselessness.
More than once he had considered raising his hand to
her when she got like that, but Colm Marsten was not
a man of bold action. He was, after all, a freedman pig
farmer from a line of freedmen pig farmers too timid
to ask for more than their little plot and to be left alone
to scratch out a living. She'd married him because her
family was poorer still, he supposed, and when their fa-
thers had arranged the match Colm had been hopeful.

Those hopes had withered away, one by one: no
dowry to speak of but two diseased pigs who died within
a fortnight (an ill omen, he mused now), no children
after twenty years of desultory and brief, late night
fumblings, generally after a night of ale.

Why had he married at all? He wondered this misera-
bly with the familiar wear of the rutted grooves of a
Roman road. And though he was not a handsome man,
there were girls in the village that sometimes caught his
eye, and he was sure he caught theirs; he thought things
of them he had to confess to the priest later or take with
himself behind the woodshed of a night when he was
sure Morag was asleep.

A cry came again; closer, sharper. A high shrill call
like a witch on the wind, rolling over the moor with
mourning and fear. He turned again, his stomach lurch-
ing. A... bird? Or…

He turned again and began walking faster. Almost running in the mud, his footfalls a muddy half-splash. Was it true what they said of this moor? Had he put his very soul at hazard trying to save himself from the sins of theft and covetousness? Did the Devil's Own prowl this place after nightfall, as the old women had always relished to say?

He rounded a bend and found a low-canopied copse of stunted trees by the roadside, scarcely thirty feet across, but it looked nominally more dry there than standing soaked in the roadway. And if something were on his trail, perhaps he could spy it out from hiding as it came around the bend... if it went on legs as a man goes. In the failing light, the shadows under the trees were deep.

He cursed himself for a fool for not bringing more than a flagon of oil for his lantern. He procured it now and then gazed up and down the road for a long moment. If he risked light, his concealment was gone. If he risked no light, he would be blind here under the trees in a short time as the very last of the daylight receded into night, and he would be in a pretty state trying to fumble with fire makings in the dark and the wet.

He decided light was better than no light and set to lighting his lantern. It was mercifully drier under the birches, and after a few minutes he had managed to light his lantern.

Two eyes like twin moons gleamed out at him from beyond the circle of light, and a wolf's mouth curled back into a snarl of white, nearly luminous fangs.

Marsten willed himself to move, felt a cry of surprise die in his suddenly parched throat, but he did not move.

Could not move.

It could be on him with a light spring. It did not spring, however. It moved forward into the light on powerful shoulders, although it was lithe and smooth and russet.

It sniffed at him, nearly nose to nose, and then loped off into the rain and toward a hilltop.

Marsten watched it go, nearly forgetting to breathe, but when it crested the hilltop and disappeared out of sight, he heard that high cry again. What was it? What did it mean?

Marsten decided he'd had enough. He rose to go, but figures were emerging from the gloom, rounding the bend from which he had come. Colm threw his cloak over the lantern, then hunkered down in fear, not sure why he knew to be seen was death but knowing it in his bones. The figures crossed from the roadside and made for the hilltop where the wolf had disappeared moments earlier. They made strange noises in their throats, low growls then high and ululating cries, almost howls, were ghostly and frightening in the witchlight.

Marsten was scarcely sure he saw it—but the clouds seemed to break open for a moment, and rays of moonlight shot down through the fog like slanting beams of pearl and fell on the figures; there were a dozen. Perhaps more and then they shed their cloaks. They were women. Women he knew. Women he recognized from the village. Elsa and Dierdre and Meredith and Katherine, old women, young women. Maids, matrons, and crones. Wrinkled, gray flesh and plump pink flesh and pert peach nipples and heavy, sagging teats perched like bits of dark stone in the chill air of the moor danced together under the moonlight, reveling in nakedness, hurling clothes away from themselves and dancing in a ring as they made their way ever onward toward the wolf's hilltop, hooting and calling and howling, their shrieks and cries freezing Marsten's blood as he watched in stark amazement. The women of the village danced and turned lascivious and wanton under the flickering shafts of moonlight that seemed to carpet their way.

It was not a conscious choice to follow when they disappeared over the rise, and he stumbled along among the heather and the bracken, the moonlight faded and the fog rose again swirling, but he could just make out the hilltop. He could not have said why, exactly, but he was impelled to see what these women, women who had warned the menfolk of the village all their lives to stay away from the Blackmoor of a night, were doing.

He crested the hill, shivering from fear as much as from cold. The rain had died away, and on top of the hill was a high fire in a wide circle of stones, and the women were dancing around it naked, except they were not women. They wore the shapes of wolves; even the russet wolf he had seen earlier in the trees now loped on two legs as a woman would walk—her shape was no longer strictly wolf nor was it a woman, but rather some unholy and demonic amalgamation, some blasphemous impure mixture procured by blackest alchemy. Staked to the opposite lip of the hilltop was a freshly dead pig. He had not heard its cries, if it had indeed had time to make any. These creatures had its blood on their jaws and claws and breasts and thighs.

There was a figure in the center of their circle, near the flames. A very old, grey-furred wolf-beast, male and engorged. They circled, kneeling and supplicating themselves, guiding him into them, then skipping off to dance again and circle and bark and howl down the fog-shrouded moon. Marsten must have gasped, or sputtered, or perhaps the stink of fear cascaded off of him in heavy clouds, but they turned as one in their frenzy. Their eyes were dull with hunger and lust, and for a moment he regarded them, and they regarded him. *They look*, he thought, *surprised*.

Then he was belting down into the dark, his lantern forgotten, panic like a gargoyle on the belfry of his mind. He raced, fell, rose, raced again, banged his knees and legs, cut himself, face hands and ankles and knees on jutting rocks, brambles, heather, racing across the moor as single-minded and terrified as a hare in its last moments of life, before the screaming starts and then stops again.

Marsten ran as if the Devil Himself and all the demons of Hell were at his heels, and in the distance, he heard their howling calls of hunting. Their growling was a sinister note in the mist. He pounded until he found the road, slipped in a puddle and fell, rose muttering and gasping, gibbering and half-mad; he begged out a prayer breathlessly and ran, and ran, and ran.

When he reached Whitby, and his own front door, Marsten nearly wept. Inside, a low fire was burning in the hearth. He came in through his door, late as it was (near to early morning now, he thought) and knelt by the fire, his head against the warm stone, and did naught but breathe for a long time. He knelt with his cold, scratched hands toward the fire, feeling the delicious sting and then the agonizing ache as the feeling returned to each finger. He heard Morag stir in the bed. He sighed relief, sobs in his throat. He whispered a prayer of gratitude to all the Saints and Martyrs that they suffered him to live and escape the Devil's grasp this night.

A russet wolf, hair just the color of Morag's, sat up in his bed, and her lips curled back into a snarl, then sprang on him. His last thought, before madness swallowed him as surely as the wolf would, was only this: *"Why did I marry?"*

CHAPTER 21

BILLY'S BAD NEWS

"You never know what worse luck your bad luck saved you from."
–No Country for Old Men, Cormac McCarthy
Tuesday evening
24 May, 2016

Nob arrived at Billy's cabin in his truck ten minutes or so behind the crows. He bounced up the ruts and potholes of the long, dirt driveway. The crows were an oily black film over every tree. Aria and Billy were standing on the porch marveling at the sudden arrival of the crows and their numbers and their silence.

Nob stuck a massive hand out the window in greeting. She wore a grey fleece bathrobe much too large for her tiny frame, and he wore only a pair of jeans. He was a well-made boy—handsome, agile, and well-muscled.

Nob sighed when he stopped the car. He reached into the glove box and came out with a silver coin. "Gods be merciful," he whispered and stepped out, shoving the coin in his pocket.

"Good evening," he said. "How are you both?"

They looked at each other, a little confused, "Uh, we're fine. Are you selling something, Mister?" asked Billy, "Because we're not—"

"No, no, nothing like that," Nob said. "I came following these birds. My name is Nob."

"Uh, well, it's a private driveway, sir," said Billy.

"This is complicated," said Nob, "but I need to speak to you... both. May I come in?"

"We're a bit busy just now," said Billy, looking at Aria to check the weather of her face.

She appeared calm but her eyes were riveted to Billy in a way that unsettled Nob. *Already it has begun*, he thought. "This is important, and I shall not be long. It's about your weekend. Do you remember it?"

Billy's mouth opened to answer but no words came. Aria looked at Billy and cocked an eyebrow, then looked at Nob as if seeing him for the first time.

Billy gestured Nob forward, "What's your name again?"

Nob strode up on the porch, ducking the eaves, tall as he was.

"Nob. And you are?" he asked, offering his hand.

"Billy Hatfield." They shook hands. Billy had a strong grip, and Nob smelled sex on both of them.

"I'm Aria," she said. "Aren't you the guy who owns *The Cauldron*?"

"Yes, hello Aria. Have you been into the shop?"

"Once or twice," she said. "And you've been to Fernwood once or twice, I think."

He nodded with a smile, "I have. Fine hamburgers they make there. Is that where you work?"

"Yeah. I pour at the bar, mostly."

"I see." They stepped inside.

"Let's talk, then," said Billy, throwing himself into a chair and gesturing for Nob to sit on the couch. "What do you know about my weekend?"

Aria went and sat beside Billy, gazing at him with something that was a mixture of adoration and naked lust.

"If it is not too forward of me to ask, how long have you two been dating?" asked Nob.

They both looked uncomfortable for a moment, "Uh... since... this afternoon..." she said with a slightly chagrined smile pulling at the corners of her lips.

"I see," he said, his fears confirmed. He tried not to let the amiable smile fall from his face. He was in more danger than he had realized. He wondered what the crows would do if things went bad. Probably pick his bones for all his trouble. Still, it had to be done.

"I've come because I know some of the Old Ways, and I have an agreement with the crows, at least for the moment. They led me here because I asked them to show me who had done the killings at Bixby Creek Bridge over the weekend."

"Killings??" said Billy, the ruddy color and heat draining from his face. "What killings?"

"Friday night, the night before the Full Moon, a couple was attacked and murdered on Bixby Creek Bridge by something tremendously strong. It fed on them. The authorities, I believe, concluded it was an animal attack. Then, on Saturday at dusk, another couple was murdered on Pfeiffer Beach, and a Park Ranger went missing. This time, whatever it was devoured the woman almost whole after knocking her van over on the road. They found the remains of the ranger half a mile away also almost wholly consumed."

"That's so gross," said Aria, "and awful, but what does it have to do with Billy?"

"I am coming to that. My guess is that Billy woke up Monday morning naked, covered in blood, no memory of the weekend." He took a deep breath and looked at the dawning horror in Billy's face, then decided just to go for it. "I'm also guess that within the last month something happened that changed you. Your senses felt more acute, your strength and stamina increased, your moods grew more powerful and strange, and you've had vivid, disturbing dreams, probably of a Great Wolf. Is this not so? You were bitten or scratched or had some sexual contact with a skin-changer. You've become a werewolf."

Aria would have laughed, but the look of fear and disgust on Billy's face made it impossible, despite the fact that what Nob was suggesting was pants-on-head crazy.

"A werewolf?" said Aria. "Come on. That's insane."

"Yes, in a way," said Nob. "But it's also true. Sanity depends on order, and indeed there is an order to this disease, which has both a physical and a spiritual component."

Billy's eyes were glazed over. He said nothing. He rose and went to the kitchen, opened the refrigerator and grabbed a bottle of water, opened, guzzled it down, reached for a second and drained it as well. He turned back. "How did you know all that?"

"I have read much of this, heard many stories. My mother was a Gothi of the Aesir in her youth, and I learned a great deal from her."

"But, how do you know about *me*?"

"Billy, you can't seriously be listening to this crackpot?" said Aria, her voice rising in alarm.

"I did wake up naked," said Billy. "Covered in blood. No memories. I did have... an experience. Something bad. A few weeks ago. But, I thought it was a dream."

"Things like this don't happen," said Aria. "It's kid stuff. Maybe you were drugged. Maybe you had a nervous breakdown and fell in the woods and hit your head. Maybe a million things that don't involve the impossible. You didn't eat five people this weekend. That's madness. This guy is wrapped up in it somehow. We should call the cops."

Billy was pale, trembling, and looked as if he would vomit.

Nob sighed, "Well, there is a way to check, but I don't like to use it."

She rounded on him, "That's *enough out of you*."

"Tell me, Aria, is it usual for you to meet a man and desire him so much and so immediately?"

"We'd met before today," she said.

"But you hadn't felt this kind of attraction earlier?" he asked.

The question brought her up short.

"No," she said quietly. "I suppose not."

"And have you acted in ways out of the ordinary in service to this feeling?" asked Nob.

"I. Maybe. Maybe I have…"

Nob nodded sympathetically. "This is a power they have, particularly around the Full Moon. They can loose the animal drives of others. Lust, rage, and fear. A skin-changer could increase the morale of a fighting unit in the Viking Days, turn them absolutely savage if they came under his sway. It appears Billy found the knack without understanding what he was doing to you—because it often takes focus to direct, as I understand it."

Aria tried to form a rebuttal, but now it was her turn to open her mouth and find she had no response. After a moment she said. "This is crazy."

"Yes," said Nob, agreeably.

Billy came and sat down in the chair across from Nob. "What's the test?"

Nob produced the silver coin and laid it on the coffee table between them, sliding it across the scored, mug-stained wood.

Billy recoiled at the shine on the thing in the fading light of day. There was a sound of fluttering wings outside, and the windows darkened as curtains of black feathers and jet-black eyes filled the windows, scratching at the glass and the roof shingles.

Aria looked from the crow-covered windows to the silver coin on the coffee table.

"Pick it up," said Nob, "But don't lose control."

Billy slapped his palm down on the coin and there was an instant smell of burning hair and flesh, a sizzle like frying bacon, and an inhuman roar of rage and pain from Billy, who jumped up so fast, pulling his hand away, that he upset the chair he was sitting in and launched himself across the room in one acrobatic leap. His hand smoked: a red, blistered circle. His face was contorting as if his bones wanted to rip through his skin. His voice was a high whine punctuated with rough, guttural growling. Aria screamed. The crows, as one, flapped and screeched and clawed the windows and disappeared into the air, as if they had never been there. The retreating evening light flooded back into the cabin.

Nob rose, pulling the coin back into his pocket and he went to Billy, whispering something in a tongue Aria did not know. Billy seemed to calm down, listening to this, his eyes far away for a moment.

He got lower, and lower, and lower, his body sagging with exhaustion. Nob gently set him down and Billy laid back against the wall, breathing slowly and evenly.

"My God," he said softly, swallowing, then went on saying it, "My God, My God, My God."

Aria went to him and looked at his hand. The impression on his hand was a perfect copy of the coin.

"You still doubt?" Nob asked her.

"No," she said. "But does this mean... you said sexual contact?"

"It's not certain with sex, unless the change is on them. But if you want you can check."

He held out the coin. Billy recoiled on the floor, "Keep that fucking thing away from me!"

"All right, all right," said Nob softly, slipping it back in his pocket.

They all breathed quietly in that space for a long time before Billy said, "So, what do we do now?"

Nob said, "You learn to control it. You don't infect others. You chain yourself up on nights you have to change. You buy raw meat wholesale. You do not, under any circumstances, murder anyone else."

"What if I already have infected someone else?" asked Billy, touching Aria's face with the unwounded hand. She leaned into him and kissed him.

"Then you must learn together."

"There's no cure?" he asked.

"There are stories. I don't believe them. Supposedly exorcism by a priest can drive out the Wolf. The tears of a loved one. Talismans to forestall the change. Potions and draughts. Personally, I've never heard of it working for real."

"But maybe there's a chance?" asked Aria.

"I would say the ship has already set sail," said Nob gently, "and now it is best to learn to live with it."

She rose, her jaw set, "Hand me the coin, please."

"Yes, of course," he said and produced it from his pocket.

She took no time to regard it but reached for it quickly then drew her hand back with a ragged scream and regarded her blistered fingers with mute, breathless horror.

LELA CLOSES UP SHOP

"We are all animals, my lady."
–Darkness, *Legend Dusk*
Tuesday
24 May, 2016

Frank had settled them into the little hotel room. He'd picked up supplies: steak and soon-to-be-baked potatoes, soon-to-be-roasted asparagus and a soon-to-be-empty bottle of red wine from the grocer. He prepared them in the kitchenette of the place, had set the table and prepared candles and was on his way out the door to pick up Lela when he got a call from Ingalls.

"Yeah?"

"Frank," he said. "I got your report. Thanks. We've put a rush in particular on the redwood crime scene. Prelim tests come back as a human male Caucasian vic, dental records of the pulled teeth lined up on the stump match Abrams, as do the hairs from the scalp. No apparent second victim but other follicles at the scene: wolf hair. Actually, get this, some kind of wolf hair that isn't a species they know of but definitely a wolf—a paleozoologist by the name of Friedman entered something similar that still isn't quite a match in a wolf database a few months ago saying it was from a find in the La Brea Tar Pits—a Dire Wolf. But those fuckers went extinct after the last Ice Age."

"That scene looks like ritual to me," said Frank, "not animal feeding. Maybe there's a cult with a weird pet. Contacted someone today talking about some weird Old Time Norse Religion stuff. I'll put it in a report. If it's a cult and they prep well, maybe they were dressed against forensics."

"Right. Be careful out there. If it's a cult, they may come for you when they guess you're on to them. You don't know how many. You want me to send you some-one to watch your back?"

"Let's see what we find in the next few days and go from there. I'll let you know."

"When are you getting a cell phone, Frank?"

"Wouldn't work around here anyway. No one has reception. Talk later, Sarge."

"Right. Out here." Ingalls hung up.

"Dire Wolf," muttered Frank, as he made his way out the door, hurrying to pick up Lela from where she must now be waiting, "Right next to the Yeti and the honest politician…"

Meanwhile…

The last of the patrons had left, and Lela had helped Mrs. Kinkaid shelve books, clear away stray pencils, crumpled papers, gum wrappers, and the usual after-hours detritus that accumulated in most libraries. Mrs. Kinkaid had locked up, saying, "If you like, dear, I can give you a ride to wherever you're staying." The old woman looked up into the gathering gloom and the empty parking lot with faint disapproval. The Fernwood Campground and the Bar and Grill were right across the street, though, with its cheerful lights burning in the dim. A black Cadillac seemed to brood there as it had for days.

"Frank'll be along any minute, Mrs. Kinkaid. Thank you," said Lela.

Mrs. Kinkaid nodded then said, "Thanks for your help today, Lela. We'll see you tomorrow." The old lady got in her '98 Buick and rolled slowly out of sight.

Darkness closed around the library and around Lela. She began to think about what Nob had said. She regarded the sky, but no moon had risen yet. It was dark and ominously quiet. Where was Frank?

Footsteps echoed from the blacktop of the road, unhurried. A swarthy, dark-eyed man in night-colored clothes materialized from the gloom across the street and regarded the Cadillac. He had close-cropped, almost buzzed black hair and a heavy coat. He walked around the Cadillac, still the only car in the lot, and wrote down the plate number on a small pad then replaced it in his pocket. Then, the dark man went inside with a light step.

Something in his movements told Lela he was a hunter on a stalk. This man was after something… or someone. She decided to write down the plate number herself… she crossed the street and wrote the number in pen on her hand, looking furtively at the door of the place, half expecting the dark man to burst out at her and… *what*? What was he going to do?

She walked to the rough but ornately-carved redwood door of the Fernwood Bar and Grill, opened it slightly, and peeped in. The dark man, who was rather cruelly handsome in the light and more than somewhat fit, was asking the bartender, "And how long has this other bartender, Aria, is it? How long has she been gone?"

"All afternoon, actually, weird, right?" said the pretty blonde waitress.

"With the owner of the Cadillac outside? What's his name?"

"Oh, that's Billy's Caddie…" said the waitress, giggling at this handsome older man. "He's a writer."

A hand came down on Lela's shoulder and she fairly jumped out of her bones. She stifled a scream but spun in terror, expecting a wolf's head and teeth and not knowing why. It was not a wolf's head though, but Frank's face that met her.

"Hey, sorry I'm late. Got a call from Ingalls. I made us some dinner. Are you ready?" he asked.

She smacked his arm. "Scared me, you shit." Then, laughing, "You made us dinner? Not Chef Boyardee, I hope."

"Nah, steak and potatoes. You know, fancy stuff. I can be fancy sometimes."

"Sounds like you're angling to get lucky," she said, taking his hand and walking out to the Parks vehicle Andy had signed out to him for the duration of the investigation.

"There was… Frank," she said, remembering what she had been doing before he startled it from her mind, "there's someone in there asking questions. About this car." She pointed to the Caddie and told him what she had seen.

"Could be nothing. It's probably nothing," he said. "Steak's getting cold."

And yet.

Frank and Lela turned and went inside.

The dark-haired man was sitting at the bar now, talking to the gentleman there, ostensibly pouring drinks, although it was all but deserted. A local or two sat in the corners, but there were no tourists, no campers. Oddly quiet, although everyone understood why without having to say *the highway is out. The summer is ruined. We may all go broke.*

Frank and Lela sat down at the bar.

"House whiskey. Neat," said Frank.

"Bulleit Bourbon okay?" asked the barman. Frank nodded. "And for the lady?"

"Moscow mule," she said. "And make sure the mule kicks."

Frank arched an eyebrow at her, holding laughter in, then he turned his attention to the dark man.

"And whatever this gentleman is drinking."

"Only club soda," said the dark man.

"I'm Frank," he said, offering his hand.

"I'm Father Giovanni de Santa Ana," said the dark-haired man with a vice-grip handshake.

"A priest? Nice to meet you, Father."

"Yes. And you. You have the air of a police officer," said Giovanni. "And you, dear lady, watched me from the library steps across the street when I came, is it not so? Then watched me from the doorway there?"

Lela blushed and, in what could not have been better timing, the bartender put her drink in front of her, which she sipped in lieu of a reply.

"Yes, I'm a detective," said Frank. "And yes, I'm here about the murders. What about you?"

"I'm here for the same reasons. The Church is concerned about a demonic influence in the tragic events over the weekend, and I have been asked to report on whether or not these concerns are justified. I tell you what most people wouldn't believe because I assume you will leave here and check on who I am and what I do, directly, like any good detective." The man seemed to have ice water in his veins. He said all this with pleasant conversationality, but his eyes were untouched by the affability of his tone.

This man was about his business, Frank decided, and he began to wonder what he had stepped into here.

"How would you judge whether a murder was influenced by demons, exactly, Father?" asked Frank.

"Well, there are many ways," said the priest. "For example, Detective, if the murderer was inhumanly strong, or able to do things normal people can't do. For example, I investigated a case in Rome some years ago wherein a witch carried the body of a woman to the top of a church, free climbing one-handed across the exterior. Witnesses said she looked like a grotesque fly."

"I don't really believe in witches," said Frank.

"Before that case, I wasn't truly sure I did, either."

"What happened?"

"I arrived and sorted it out. She can't hurt anyone anymore. God help her poor soul."

"That sounds a bit like a murder confession."

"Not at all. She lives in a sanatorium in the Apennines, but she is still tortured by what she has done."

"What do you think happened here over the weekend, Father?" asked Lela.

"I'm not certain yet," he said with a soft smile. "But when I know more, I'll be happy to discuss the matter with you, to the extent the Church allows me to do so."

"Where are you staying, Father?" asked Frank.

"Big Sur River Inn," said the priest. "Room 11. Drop by if you want to compare notes some time, Detective."

"Why were you eyeing that Cadillac?" asked Lela.

"It's an attractive car, isn't it?" asked the priest. "In a nostalgic, Americana way…"

"That's why you needed the plate number?" asked Frank.

"Is that an official question? Am I being detained?"

"No," said Frank, "but I'd like to know."

The priest opened his notebook and tore out a page, laid it on the bar, and said, "Goodnight, Detective. Goodnight, Ma'am."

He walked out the door, and Frank and Lela looked at the torn page on the bar. It was a rough but startlingly accurate sketch of Lela, a frightened look on her face, standing alone in the dark hollow of the library stairway to the parking lot. The priest had faced away from her when he drew this sketch.

Frank shot his bourbon and said, "Let's go eat dinner, screw, and then run this Cadillac plate outside, if only to find out why he had an interest and didn't want to say so."

She giggled, swatted his arm again, "I don't like that word. Screw."

"How do you feel about the idea, though?"

"Play your cards right and you might find out, Mister," she said.

CHAPTER 23:
NO PLACE LIKE LONDON

London, England
Summer, 1824

Bethany had worked as a bangtail in Whitechapel since she was 14, when her mother had died of the cholera. In the three years since, she had managed to scratch out a living, drifting between taverns of dark reputation and her shabby garret with the sort of gentlemen as would pay for her company. She had always been beautiful. Even under the greasepaint and the rouge, she stood apart from others. Rose Powers had once, in what Bethany assumed was jealousy and drunkenness, decided to try to smash in "that pretty nose of yours, my girl."

Bethany, ten years younger and ten pounds lighter, had sidestepped her haymaker and pushed her hard in the back. Rosy Powers went careening headfirst into an adjacent alley wall and lost two teeth for her trouble. The men didn't mind about Rose's teeth; they didn't look at her face much anyway. Bethany's face, though, was what paid for the room she kept that was (and she was fiercely proud of this) her own.

The men sometimes asked her to call them father, or pretend to be their mother, or to say things that turned her stomach, but they were always riveted on her face. Her blue eyes and blonde hair, full lips, her height, and her pale, clear skin attracted attention the other "ladies of the evening" could not boast—whatever tricks they knew.

One summer night, though, something happened that changed things. Changed everything.

It had been a particularly wet year, and in the spring, there had been a gale that nearly ripped the roof off of her little place. Repairs had been slapdash, and she'd been working harder than usual to earn enough to really repair the roof before the onset of winter.

Bethany and a few of the others generally worked Fairclough Street from Back Church to Christian Streets. There was a warm summer drizzle and she walked beneath the eave. Bethany had declined to work at a brothel because she didn't care to share her wages. Pimps had approached her to put her under contract, but she had managed, thus far, to remain independent through a series of lucky breaks (for example, it had been her good fortune that when Roy Norton threatened to fuck her with a knife if she didn't agree to work for him, someone bashed his brains out with a length of pipe the next night at the Old Rose in a drunken argument).

So, Bethany walked the dangerous streets of Whitechapel all but alone that winsome and wet evening in the summer of 1824. It was not uncommon for crowds of streetwalkers to mob men, caressing and entreating them in the very street, but Bethany was not among them. She waited, at least, until she was approached to begin a transaction. Her beauty meant she never waited long, but tonight the roiling, roistering, pestilent neighborhood was rather quiet.

That was when a beautiful young man with dark, tousled curls falling across his face appeared out of the darkness of a side street shouldering a leather bag, looking harried and, perhaps, fearful. He had gray eyes and generous lips, though he was slender as a fresh-ground knife blade. His movements were lithe and graceful, and he walked toward her with controlled urgency.

"Please, let's walk together, Miss," he said softly and low, offering his arm.

She allowed herself to be turned and slipped her arm through his, setting off the way she had come with this achingly beautiful young man. He wore a gentleman's attire and spoke in a refined manner that nevertheless could not hide the hint of a foreigner's accent, although she couldn't quite place it. Periodically he would glance furtively over his shoulder. She quoted him a price quietly and lightly, as if commenting on the weather, and he agreed at once, saying only, "Have you a place we might go to get off the street?" Another look over his shoulder.

"Yes," she said, "but are we running from someone?"

"No," he said, but his face was almost frightened.

He mopped his brow, and she was sure there was sweat mingled with the rainwater beading there. For a moment, she gauged that he was younger than she had at first guessed. Perhaps twenty. No older, certainly, than twenty-two. His cheeks were ruddy. Had he been running?

A horse and trap clattered by, punctuated by the clip-clop of hooves on the cobblestone street. The young man abruptly guided her gently (but with considerable strength) into an alcove, and holding her slender waist, he put her back to the street, his own to a shop door. He kissed her somewhat clumsily then but with endearing tenderness and sincerity, enfolding her in an embrace. One hand slipped to the bag he carried until it passed.

He has never done this before, she realized, *and something has him terrified.* Instinct told her two things that pulled in different directions then. One, he was wealthy enough and naive enough to pay for the roof over his head tonight, if she played it right. Two, he was in danger and so would she be for as long as they were together.

In her garret, he laid his bag carefully by the bedside table while she lit candles and helped him out of his clothes with gentle fingers. It was unusual for her to find her clients attractive, but this young man was (had she known it) something Michelangelo might have sculpted. It was with curious pleasure she undressed him by firelight. The only blemish was a relatively fresh brand on his inner bicep; a cruciform sword and beneath it the words *Deus Vult.*

She wanted to ask about it. She suddenly wanted his name and his story and to know what had him so frightened, and whether or not (as she suspected) this was his first time, but her time in the trade had taught her not to pry. She laid him on her freshly-made bed.

He kept eyeing the windows until she pulled the curtains, then slowly undressed for him, as she had learned gentleman liked for her to do. He responded in the usual way. They transacted in the usual way. The outcomes were as usual, although Bethany found (rather unusually for her) that she had also taken great pleasure in this boy's body as he had in hers.

They lay together for a time. Then he said, "That was beautiful. Thank you. You will never know what it meant to me."

She nearly laughed, curled under his arm, at his sincerity. This was a boy in a man's body.

"I'm pleased you were pleased. Perhaps you'd like it again," she said, curling her fingers around his long, dark locks.

"I would," he said. "But... I should go. I've stayed too long already."

"If you're sure," she said, sliding her hands down his torso.

"I. I've never been with a woman before. I took vows."

"Oh, vows?" she said sweetly, her hand slipping further down his body.

"Yes. I was a priest. Or am a priest. I don't know…"

"A Catholic?" she asked, amused. This would be a first for her.

"Yes, I was raised in a monastery in Dordogne. Abandoned by my mother. They took me in. They groomed me. Taught me to... taught me what I know."

"And now you've come to London," she said, running her nails up and down his smooth thighs with painful, delightful slowness. He shivered and gooseflesh rose on his arms.

"Y-es," he breathed and rolled to kiss her. They transacted again.

When she awoke, the rain had begun again and there was a steady *drip, drip, drip* into the pans and buckets she had laid about the garret. His warmth and scent filled the bed, and she luxuriated in it. Their passion had been something unusual in her experience, though she often affected passion. It was not like her to fall asleep with a lover, *client*, she corrected herself.

The candles had almost burned themselves out when she suddenly heard a faint *scratch, scratch, scratch* at the door.

A low, rumbling voice accompanied the smell of musk tinged with rusty-penny blood and wet animal hair, "Priiiiiieeeest," it growled.

"Cooooommmeee ouuuuut, priiiieeessst. Weeeee knoooow you're heeere, priest. We've come for your *blood and bones*." This last word was almost a sharp bark, as of great jaws slamming shut on the last syllables.

She felt him roll slowly and quietly to the bedside table and slide open his leather bag and produce a strangely ornate Lefaucheux pinfire revolver inscribed with the cross and, it appeared, plated in acid-etched silver. Very carefully and quietly, he unfolded the trigger from the body of the weapon, pulled back the hammer and aimed it at the door, rising. He did not take his eyes from the door as he climbed naked from the bed but put a finger to his lips and gestured that she should hide.

"What kept you, Killian?" he said.

"I smell a girl in there with you, priest. What *have* you been doing? What would the *Gladius* say?" came the menacing growl behind her door.

"I've renounced it. Renounced it all, Killian. I want to live in peace. I want no more killing," he said.

"Why, Gaspard. You already took the vows," replied the *thing* behind the door that Bethany was increasingly certain was not human. She climbed under the bed but not before she teased out a straight razor from beneath the mattress. "And you already killed my own kin."

"I ask God to forgive me," said Gaspard quietly.

"If you've no stomach for killing, and if you trust God, put down that little French fist gun, lad, and open the door."

"Go away, Killian," said Gaspard, "or as God is my judge, you'll die tonight."

"You can't escape the life you chose, Gaspard," said the monstrous voice in a curiously sorrowful tone.

"Then let us meet in the street," Gaspard said evenly, but every knotty sinew of his body tensed, and thick ropes of muscle corded over his naked form in anticipation of what came next. The door shattered inward and a black wolfman lunged through it, two others at his flanks, one a dusky gray color and the other a dark brown.

Gaspard squeezed off a shot that caught the dark brown one, the smallest of the three, in the throat and the force of the round slammed the creature into the wall, cracking the plaster of Paris and splattering fragments of jawbone from wall to ceiling. It screamed a cry and slumped silently against the wall, unblinking.

Gaspard managed another shot that whizzed by the black one's ear (Killian? Bethany was sure the black one was the one he had called Killian). Then, they were both on him, and the revolver was spinning away, crashing into the window and then, falling to hook precariously on the jagged windowsill. There were horrific screams of pain, animal snarls like ripping fabric, growling, candles knocked over, wood splintering, glass breaking, and then her bed was hurled against the wall and the one called Killian snatched her up.

She swatted at him with the straight razor, opening a gash in his arm before he swatted it away and slammed her back down by the neck. She convulsed on the floor, fighting for breath, the room going gray, his snarling maw like a widening tunnel.

Gaspard was screaming as the gray wolf held him down, "Let her go! Leave her alone! STOP IT, KILLIAN! IN the NAME of GOD, STOP!"

"Oh, no, Gaspard," said Killian, quietly, "I'm afraid she is a part of your punishment."

While the young priest watched, they took from her roughly and with cruelty what they had not transacted for. When they were through, they tossed her limp body to the opposite wall where she cracked her head, spider webbing the plaster with a punctuation mark of scarlet in the outline of her shape. She groaned softly in agony. Gaspard, well past madness, screamed and thrashed, and wept and then went strangely still as Killian knelt before him, opening his great right paw and splaying his claws.

"Now you die, Gladius Dei. You die a faithless priest, hell-bound, and in despair. Your little harlot will be one of us by the next Moon." He stretched out a clawed hand toward Gaspard's throat when the first bullet ripped through the back of his skull, the second came in behind the ear, and the third and fourth went into the gray wolfman's left and right eyes as he looked up in shock at Bethany, who stood with the Lefaucheaux in her bloody fist, a look of unvarnished hatred on her purpling face. Both creatures slumped and began to diminish into men, pale and paunchy and blood-spattered.

Bethany collapsed, then crawled slowly to Gaspard, who said first, "Forgive me."

She realized she probably could not but said nothing.

"We must go. There will be more soon. And someone will come looking for what the noise was about."

In the desolation of her thoughts, in her shock, this she understood. She, limping haltingly, slipped on something barely decent, snatched the purse under the bathroom floorboards where she kept her money, and wandered out into the hall as the sound of approaching feet pounded up the front stairs. Gaspard recovered the gun, his clothes, his bag, and they slipped out the back stairway and into the night.

In the morning, with fresh clothes and new names, Gaspard and Bethany (who signed the Ship's register as Remy and Catherine Duplechain) took a berth on the *Diana* outbound for New Orleans, where Gaspard said he had a brother who had prospered and could help them.

And so the Strain came to the New World.

CHAPTER 24:
THOUGHT AND MEMORY

Tuesday Night
May 24, 2016

Billy sat on the back porch of the cabin for a long time after Aria left for home. They hadn't been able to find his wallet or the keys to his Cadillac, and they had arranged for a tow truck and re-keying in the morning. He had cancelled his credit cards and re-ordered what he could over the phone, and now he sat thinking. Brooding, he mused, might be a better word. Brooding on his own curse.

But that was too dramatic for him. Too angsty and teenaged, it smacked of self-pity, and he pushed it away. Nob had stayed, and Billy was grateful for it; the tall man had brought bad news, but he also brought sympathy. He had not judged Billy harshly for what appeared to be a number of grisly murders charged to his account, or at least the account of the wolf he had become over the weekend. He also had not pried into how Billy came to be infected. Instead, he had been kind and approached the subject with gentle good humor, such as he might. At the moment, Nob was inside making a meal.

"It's important to eat when things are bad," the big man had said, and began chopping an onion and crushing garlic. Whatever he was cooking smelled great. Aria had begged off, saying she needed to be on her own to think but that she would be back. Probably tonight.

Nob stepped out to the porch.

"How are you, Bill?" asked Nob.

"Bill? Only my mother calls me Bill," he chuckled. Then, after a moment, he said, "I'm okay. I mean, my hand hurts, but…"

"More ice?" asked Nob.

"No. I don't know. This thing is too big, man."

"My mother would say 'Small strokes fell great oaks.' It sounds better in Norwegian."

"Your mother is Norwegian?" asked Billy.

"Yes. Both my parents. I grew up there."

"How did you end up here?" asked Billy.

"It's not a story I tell often," said Nob, "but it is something you might be interested to hear."

"Okay," said Billy, "go for it."

Nob regarded the dark woods outside and said, "It's a better story inside of doors after dark. Come, let's have dinner."

They sat down to pasta Alfredo, garlic bread, white wine, and steamed broccoli in the cabin's little kitchen where Nob's size seemed almost to double as if he sat in the miniature chairs of a dollhouse. He gripped knife and fork daintily as he began.

"So, I traveled for many years," Nob began, "left home at 16 and saw Europe, the Middle East, Northern Africa, parts of South America, East Asia, Australia, and finally North America. I was a collector, of sorts, of books and things. My family was well off, and when I found something I thought was worthwhile, I sent it back in a package or a steamer trunk or, sometimes, by the truckload. Mostly old books. Books about magic, or strange happenings, or the occult, or forgotten peoples, dark religions, and so forth.

"My mother had raised me to respect history, and she had knowledge of the Old Religion, of worship of the Aesir, the gods of the ancient North Men. Those famous old ones like Thor, Odin, and Loki, whom you probably know, and many others besides whom few people remember. Mani, god of the Moon, for example. After the Second Great War, my mother had turned her back on Christianity in her anger at the Church for its complicity in the great killing of the Jews. She turned to older ways, and she taught me much, though never forced it on me.

"When I had traveled far and long, I went home. Back to Norway when it was in the teeth of winter. My mother and father were happy to see me, but they said there was trouble in the village near our home in the country and that it was strange that I came back when I did. What sort of trouble, I asked? A killer, my father told me, has been preying on people who walk alone at night. A *varulv*, my mother said. My father scoffed. He did not believe in such things, but although I had never seen any evidence of the supernatural, I also knew that my mother was not prone to idle talk. Our differences had driven me across the world in my youth.

"That night, they showed me something that still makes me smile to remember: all of the packages, the trunks full of junk and treasure, all the artifacts and trinkets and fetishes and amulets and volumes, all of them were neatly together in a dedicated section of our library, on display under glass or on the great shelves there. I was inordinately pleased—my mother had curated these out of love for me and as a gift for my return. She was sure I would return, although I was not sure I ever would until I went.

"There had indeed been killings in the village. Of the sort you may be familiar with. Every full moon, sometimes two walking at dusk along the river, or a farmer out checking his sheep wouldn't come back. They'd find a ruined corpse, or they'd find nothing at all sometimes. The police couldn't find anything of use. They set a curfew and doubled patrols, but it came to naught. Stories of evil spirits, witches, trolls, and werewolves went out from the village to every corner of the country.

"Then, late one night, my mother woke me. She bade me follow her quietly downstairs. She wore a dark cloak and strange white robes. I did not like the look in her eyes, which were always the color of a winter sky. But I followed. I am haunted still by what came after.

"We walked out that night, a night of the full moon, and our feet found a farmhouse three miles upland. My mother had a key, though how she got it I had no idea. Inside, it all looked normal enough, but there was a heavy padlock on the basement door. She smashed it in with a hammer, and that's when I heard the animal sounds, smelled that musky lion house smell of a big predator.

"A *varulv*, patchy and gray and very, very old, with stringy muscles and bloodshot, yellowing eyes was laying there on a patch of fresh hay, breathing stertorously. I started to speak, but my mother rounded on me fiercely and hissed *Quiet, be still, and watch.*

"I obeyed. Even when she went over to it, and its eyes rolled at her with something like impotent hate and helpless terror. This was a werewolf so old it could not hunt. Could not be the one doing the killing.

"*This I do for you*, she said to me, and then she took a dagger from the belt of her robe and slit the creature's throat, proclaiming that this was a sacrifice to Odin, and in exchange she asked the favors of Thought and Memory and protection from Fenrir's Children on her only son. I stood in mute, paralyzed horror at what she had done, and when the sickly old wolf dissolved into an old woman, a woman who I realized I had known all my life as Mrs. Larsen, I fled into the night.

"She was dying, of course, of very old age. She must have been centuries old. At the time, it all seemed too monstrous, but not so monstrous as what came next.

Running into the woods, frightened almost into madness at what I had seen, trying to make sense of the familiar turned wicked and strange, I didn't see the shadow lope from the night forest or the shifting darkness in the trees. I was running, hysterical for home, and from there anywhere else away from blood and death and the dark Old Ways and dark Old Names.

"The wolfman was on me in seconds, but I never heard it coming. This was the one who *had* been doing the killings. A skin-changer who was probably so young in his Moons he didn't even realize what he was yet. So I tell myself. But in the seconds before it killed me and ate me whole, three things happened at once. A high wail came from the direction of Mrs. Larsen's house, and my mother darted across the road toward us. The wind picked up and suddenly roared through the trees, gale-force, pushing back the wolf from where it loomed over me as I lay prone, and from the trees, *thousands* of ravens descended from the trees in a nearly endless stream, calling and crying as one great bird, and they set upon the werewolf with terrible bites and scratches, their weight as they flew and crashed into him like a black fist aided by the high wind. When the beast fell, howling in pain and rage, swatting at the ravens, fairly screaming in terror, the birds set upon it and pecked until blood came, then pecked the bloody spots, until the whole animal was a writhing, ragged wound, eyeless, lipless, black with birds and red with gore.

"I did not wait to see what came next but ran for home. My mother stopped before the creature, and I assumed she would do for it as she had done for Mrs. Larsen.

"In the morning I had packed, and went into my parents' bedroom to see my father and say goodbye. A man in the shape of my father without lips or eyes, with ragged beak-holes and torn flesh where the skin of his face should have been lay unconscious in their huge bed, my mother seated primly beside him, her eyes wet. I would have screamed, but I had no breath.

"She told me she had done what she did to protect me, that Odin's Ravens would protect me, my blood for Mrs. Larsen's, and that father would recover in time, that the *varulv* will not die even from such wounds as these. That he had been infected not long ago, and that they were all 'adjusting.' That we must all 'adjust.' That years ago, it would have been honorable. My father (an account executive at a major bank) would have had pride of place as a baar-sarker among the warriors who went a-Viking. It sounded like a brass drumbeat of rationalization. Anyone might be killed during this 'adjustment,' but so long as her son was safe, it did not matter who was killed. I said some terrible things and left, swearing never to return to Norway. I never have."

Nob drank down his glass of white wine in one go and looked into Billy's face, gone vaguely green and pale.

"Jesus," said Billy, "that's some story."

"Yes," said Nob, "some story. I wandered then, for a time. The ravens and the crows come to me when there is danger from one of Fenrir's children."

"Who is Fenrir?"

"He's the Great Wolf. Son of Loki. The one who will kill Thor and eat the world when the last battle, comes at the end of all things, called Ragnarok."

"Do you believe this?" asked Billy.

"I believe stories come from somewhere. I believe there are powers in the world. The North Men called some of them Odin, Loki, Fenrir, Thor, Hel. The Romans called some of them Jupiter, Hades, Apollo, Pan, Diana. Are they the same? I don't know. Maybe not. Stories are a kind of magic and carry their own power. But I have seen strange things in my life. I expect to see more."

"Where did you go when you left Norway?"

"I traveled again, but I was haunted by what I knew, and if reports of an animal attack or a missing person reached me, I fled again. Finally, I came to Big Sur and found it beautiful, peaceful, remote, and pleasant. I decided to settle here. I opened the bookstore down by the river. Within the month, a truck rolled into the parking lot with all I had collected over the years, though I never wrote to my mother or called to ask her for any of it. And something else. She sent a wrought-iron cauldron. I renamed the bookstore *The Cauldron* and expanded it from a bookstore to an occult bookstore and novelty shop—I suppose as an attempt to make peace with my mother and make peace with the past and perhaps understand what had happened and what it meant. I have lived quietly since then, but always I have waited, expecting something like this. It feels like destiny, my friend. And I believe I am here to try to help you... if you will let me."

Billy's face was somber, and he nodded slowly, "I'm glad we met, Nob."

"I wish it were under better circumstances, Bill," said Nob.

They finished the meal in silence.

CHAPTER 25:
LAB RESULTS (AND OTHER THINGS) COME BACK

Wednesday morning
25 May, 2016

"Just talked to dispatch. Plates come back to a Billy Hatfield. Address is Mariposa County. Foresta. Near Yosemite," said Frank over the breakfast table.

Lela sipped her coffee. "Anything on that priest? Santa Ana?" she asked.

"No record. DMV has an address out of a rectory in San Francisco," said Frank.

"Wait, Billy Hatfield, did you say?" she asked.

"Yeah, why? You know him?"

"There's a writer named Billy Hatfield who lives in the Sierras. We have some of his stuff in the Library."

"What does he write?"

"Well, I think his first book was True Crime. Something about murders in the 20s, if I remember correctly. It was called…" her brow wrinkled for a moment, "I think it was called *The Hutchins Killings*. Some grisly spree up in Nebraska one winter. They never caught the serial killer. Apparently, Hatfield shed some new light on the case. FBI took another look at it, if I remember correctly," she said.

"So, a crime writer who writes about grisly murder sprees shows up in town just as some grisly murders happen. Back in the Sheriff's Office you know what they call that?" He smiled at her with the air of a man who knows a great joke.

"What?" she asked, sighing indulgently.

"They call that a clue," he said happily.

She rolled her eyes. "No law of diminishing returns on that one," she muttered.

"Every detective should be issued a librarian wife," he said, kissing her.

There was a knock at the door. Frank checked the window then said, "It's Andy."

Lela pulled her robe closer around herself as Frank opened.

"If you'd just get a cell phone, this would all be much easier," said Andy. "Just got this and Ingalls asked me to deliver it to you. Fresh, steaming lab reports, you Luddite." He handed several printed sheets over, and Frank perused them.

"Multiple victims at the Abrams scene. DNA for two, one is Abrams, one unknown, but not the victims from

Pfeiffer Beach. Wolf hair at the scene *from two different wolves*? That's… hmm." He thought for a moment, then said, as if to himself, "An additional victim. The scalp and the teeth belonged to Abrams for sure. The other was probably consumed."

"What kind of creature could eat over two hundred pounds of human flesh, bone, hair, teeth, skull, and all at a sitting?" asked Andy. "And why go to the trouble of yanking teeth and hair from one victim and not the other?"

"Well, maybe they disposed of one set of teeth and a scalp somewhere else," said Frank. "Another site we haven't found yet. Or maybe because there were two, one of them is a picky eater. It has the look of ritual to me. Maybe a cult with a couple of wolves, and they starve them for a week before they sic 'em on someone."

"There had been no old blood or anything at the scene?" asked Lela.

"No, nothing," said Frank, paging through the reports. "Why?"

"Well, if it *was* a cult ritual," she said, *or a werewolf's accustomed habit*, she thought then pushed the thought away, "then, they've maybe done this before just this way. If they didn't do it at that spot, they would have done it at others—others no one ever found. Or, if they found it, they never lived to tell about it. There can't be *that* many places with appropriately large stumps, seclusion, concealment, and close enough to a hunting ground to move struggling or unconscious victims without difficulty, can there?"

Andy nodded, "No," he said. "There can't be many. Maybe a few dozen, tops, within ten miles or so. Probably fewer. I can talk to some of my rangers. I'm pretty familiar with the backcountry. I know a few places we might look, but there are other guys I can talk to."

"Lela," said Frank, "Can you pull whatever Hatfield has written for me?"

"If you had a phone, you could probably read download samples from Amazon right now," said Lela with a smirk, "but sure. I suppose."

"Thank you," he said. "I'll let you be in charge of the evil internet boxes. I'm an analog man in a digital wasteland."

"You poor thing," she said flatly.

"Right, good thing it doesn't create work for other people," said Andy, stepping outside into cool, clean morning air.

Frank followed. "So, you'll look for other sites. I'll go in with Lela and see what I can learn about this writer."

"Right," Andy said. "I'll catch up with you later. I'll see if anyone knows where Hatfield is staying. His car is still in front of Fernwood… or was when I passed this morning."

"Let's get it towed, and he can come to us. I want him detained when he comes for that Caddie." said Frank.

"Good call," said Andy, already walking away.

CHAPTER 26:

BETHANY AND GASPARD IN THE CRESCENT CITY

New Orleans, Louisiana
April 10, 1834

Bethany, under the name Gypsy Calhoun, had become the Madame of a high-end brothel on Royal Street. Gaspard's brother, Laurent, owned an indigo plantation a few miles outside the city, and he had quietly fronted them the money to buy the extravagant, sumptuous bordello known as *Le Petite Mort*. Gaspard went under the name Charles Calhoun, played Bethany's husband, and tended bar. Three nights a month, Gypsy and Charles disappeared, none knew where, and always returned either pale, wan, and morose, or almost feverish with ruddy good health and good cheer.

That April evening, the night of the New Moon, the champagne had flowed abundantly. "The Revel," as

Bethany called it privately to Gaspard, never ended here—the girls were entertainers all, for dancing, singing, conversation, the playing of instruments, or of sexual exploits of note, even in a city renowned for such stories. The gentlemen flowed in and out like the tides of a flesh-hungry and whiskey-seasoned sea. Gaspard poured and Bethany mingled, and they chatted and danced, and that night there were no calls to deal with rowdy drunks or men who liked their beds bloody and their whores full of fear, nor (*mercifully*, thought Bethany) had they had to arbitrate the disputes, ranging from unkind words to razorblades, that occasionally arose between the women in their employ.

It was, or had been, a rather pleasant evening. An evening in which they could almost forget what they had done two weeks before when the moon was round and full and white and high, stirring their veins with fury and hunger and what they would do again in two weeks when she called the wolves in them. Gaspard, had, of course been infected simply by dint of remaining Bethany's lover, though he hadn't known, and the *Gladius Dei* hadn't prepared him for the possibility that such a thing could take place.

It hadn't seemed relevant when he was a priest, he mused from behind the bar, watching the room. He watched Bethany charming a table of poker-playing dandies bedecked and bedraped with the graceful arms, busts, waists, and smooth legs of the whispering, caressing girls who urged them ever onward, ever away to an upstairs room when the game might allow, and before their hoped-for wages were lost to the pot.

It was a fire in his very blood to look at her. After they made love for the first time after... after what had happened in London... she had taken on a luminous quality for him. Something about her was beyond just beautiful, as she had been when they had met. She was intoxicating the way goddesses in the old stories were intoxicating. Bethany, for him, was as irresistible, as achingly needful as breaths of air or droplets of rain for lips parched bloody, thirsting near unto death. It reached beyond obsession, and he knew somehow without considering it or putting it into words, that she had passed it on to him. That he was her creature but that they were both creatures of the Wolf now. Creatures of the Moon. The Children of Diana, as Bethany had put it once in their moonlit bedchamber when they were curled together, glistening with sweat like dewdrops in the pale late, writhing and orgasmic.

Watching her now, he wanted it again. Wanted her again. Wanted to pull her away from the din and the boiling life of the brothel with its oriental rugs, its burgundy velvet curtains, its dark leather couches. Wanted to find a room or a dark place in one of the halls, and to worship her with his mouth until she went rigid and gasped and ran her hands again through his long curls.

But then the stranger arrived... and the trouble began.

He wore a black wool gambler's hat with a rattlesnake skin hatband and bellied up to the bar. He was swarthy, five days unshaven with midnight black hair long in the sideburns, and Gaspard took him for a Spaniard. He had a pale horizontal slash across his throat that almost went from ear to ear, and a regular pattern of dots above and below it—someone had slit his throat, and someone had stitched him up. He radiated menace, and Gaspard smelled blood on him. He saw Bethany's head snap to the bar, and she met Gaspard's eyes for the briefest moment. They had come to recognize trouble without the need of the wolf's senses, but they could smell the danger on this man, and the wolf told them that undercurrent of blood was fresh, although the man and his attire were unblemished.

"Bourbon," said the stranger with a deep rumble, his mouth full of Spanish vowels dragged through gravel, "a bottle."

"Start a tab or pay as you go, Mister?" asked Gaspard.

"A tab," he said. "I plan to stay."

"Welcome to *La Petite Morte*, m'sieu," said Gaspard.

The stranger poured himself a drink and grinned. His front tooth was gold. Out of the corner of his eye, he saw Felice, one of the ladies of the house, start toward them, but Bethany intercepted her, whispered something in her ear, and then came to the Spaniard's side by the bar, her face a mask.

"Sir," she said. "How may we help you tonight?" she asked. Gaspard's heart fluttered at the fresh wave of her scent and marveled at the grace of her neck as it curved into shoulder and delicate collarbones and décolletage.

The Spaniard shot his bourbon and looked at her leeringly.

"You're the one they call Gypsy Calhoun, si?"

"That's my name," she said. "And you, sir?"

"My name is Santiago Vega," he said. "I am a guest of Madame LaLaurie."

She regarded him doubtfully. This man did not look like the guest of a socialite gentlewoman and certainly not Delphine LaLaurie, the owner of one of the largest homes in the *Vieux Carré*, a home which loomed not far from *La Petite Morte*, in point of fact.

"I see," she said. "Well, you are welcome here. Have you come only for refreshment or are you also interested in companionship this evening?"

He eyed her, performing almost a dumb show of lasciviousness, and when he had satisfied himself on all she might have to offer, he shrugged, "I'm looking for someone... *darker* and *younger*," he said.

Her smile flattened, and her eyes took on a dead quality, "Our girls are youthful and vivacious, but we don't employ children here, Mister Vega."

He shot another shot, although he wasn't even slightly tipsy yet, Gaspard judged. He had learned the signs. This man was not drinking to loosen, and drinking was not loosening him. He was a coiled spring compressing.

"Of course," he said. Another shot of bourbon went down his throat, and he leered at her. "I see. You like to hide what this place is."

"What is that supposed to mean?" she asked, her face flushing now.

Gaspard could smell the wolf in her rising. His own began to rise in answer. He fought it down as he was sure she must be doing as well; this was *not* the place or the time. If they changed here, there would be the Devil to pay. Their time in New Orleans would most surely be over, and the story would fly hundreds of miles in every direction. He fought the itch, the sensation of hair like goose flesh rising under his skin. His mouth suddenly felt too small for his teeth, but he pushed it away.

"I only mean," said Vega, "that you want to pretend this isn't a place where you peddle flesh, or that you only peddle *certain* flesh. That makes you *better* than those houses of low character whose girls haven't begun bleeding yet, does it? Makes you *cleaner*?"

"You're welcome to seek your company where you will. What you are looking for is not under this roof, sir," she said coldly.

He slapped her with the suddenness of a striking snake. Her head snapped to the right and blood trickled from her lip. Gaspard was over the bar with his right hand around the Spaniard's throat in an instant. The music and the din of the party stopped. Conversation stopped.

"*Out*," said Gaspard in what was almost a whisper, as clear and sure as death. The Santiago Vega's face was reddening now, his eyes bulging as Gaspard squeezed his larynx closed, knowing he could crush the throat, snap the spine, roar into the jugular and feast, and rip and…

Bethany put a hand on his shoulder and whispered, "Show him out, Gaspard." She applied her handkerchief to her lip and turned to the assemblage of customers and employees. She was a marvel, as sunny and gay as a spring morning—infectiously so.

"Strike up the music! Don't let's let one bad apple spoil the barrel. Who needs a drink? Champagne for everyone, on the house."

Gaspard felt the Spaniard (rather than saw) reaching for the knife in his vest, and his left hand found the man's groin, squeezing with the same pressure he'd kept around the man's gagging throat and walked him out. Santiago's boots kicked two inches above the ground, and he went rigid, his face looking like an overripe grape ready to pop. Gaspard hurled him into the street where the man lay for some time before he stood, straightened, and limped away toward Storyville with revenge in his eyes.

The party continued for some hours, and the atmosphere was no worse for a moment's unpleasantness earlier in the night. Gaspard had excused himself to their private courtyard to find his calm again and returned smoking a cigar—Bethany loathed even his occasional cigar smoke, but on this occasion, she was grateful he hadn't murdered the man on general principle. She knew Gaspard had grown protective in part because of what she sometimes called "their condition."

Nevertheless, she understood they loved one another, and they leaned together against the storm raging in their blood. But (and she had made her peace with this long ago) Gaspard would always be in her thrall, and it would fall to her to guide his wild love of her in ways that did not destroy them both. Despite the cigar, when he returned, she had gone to him and kissed him sweetly. They said no words, but he folded her under his arm and kissed her forehead three times. Then she crossed the room and continued to orchestrate "The Revel."

Later, many of the gentlemen had retired with the ladies of the house, and the candles were burning low. The music was softer now; someone was playing a Nocturne on the piano, and many of the inebriates had set their feet toward home when it happened.

There came screams from up the street, and rushing feet, and the roar of distant flames feeding on some great structure. "FIRE! FIRE! FIRE AT THE LALAURIE HOUSE! FIRE!"

Men were running with buckets of water. Gaspard grabbed a bucket and went to the hand pump then rushed out into the orange glow of the fire-rilled dark, the faint smell of smoke rising like a fetid, greasy fog.

The papers would report later on the horrors of the LaLaurie house; even in a community that embraced and profited by slavery, the cruelty and murder that Madame LaLaurie visited on her slaves was nothing short of legendary... and diabolical. The fire, the story went, was set by a slave who had been chained to the stove in the kitchen and who dreaded being taken to a room upstairs from which no one ever returned.

Gaspard never saw Santiago Vega appear from the alley as he rushed toward the fire, never saw him step into the emptying bordello with a shotgun under his long coat. Never heard him empty it into Bethany's skull, nor heard the kerosene lantern smash into the bottles of liquor at the bar, nor saw the flames lick up the wall as if they had a mind of their own.

By the time the fires on Royal Street were quelled, the horror of what had gone on at the LaLaurie mansion eclipsed a burned bordello or the death of Gypsy Calhoun. It was as Gaspard had learned from the *Gladius Dei* long ago: the complete destruction of a body by fire kills even a demon wolf, kills even a Child of Diana.

In his rage and fury, Gaspard sought for the Spaniard, but it would be years before he found Santiago Vega, and they would be far from New Orleans then.

CHAPTER 27:
ARIAS AND NOCTURNES

Tuesday Night on into Wednesday morning
25 May, 2016

She had left Billy's place the night before to clear her head, but distance had only made her cloudier. She had sped away, hoping to return to her own life, but thoughts of him kept filling the spaces where other ideas and priorities had always been. She had a distant impression of her job, of her roommates and what they would ask, of her parents and dinner on Sunday. Very far away, although she did not know it, the idea of returning to the East Coast and attending Sarah Lawrence was detaching itself entirely from her range of possibilities. To be so distant from Billy might as well have been distance from her limbs, but this resynthesis was still below the surface, growing like a fever she had not yet noticed. She flew down Highway One, south toward the house she rented with two others. She did not know how to address their questions, or how to explain her bandaged fingertips, but she juddered inside with the reality of how *different* everything was now.

The engine of her little Honda, growling down under the hood, sounded like standing next to the giant speakers at some epic death metal concert. The fumes were nearly overpowering, and she had to roll down the windows to keep from retching. The ridges of the steering wheel under fingertips felt almost distractingly fascinating and intense. She felt, she had to admit, powerfully alive. Powerfully sensual and even sexual. Somehow she resisted the urge to turn the car around, go back to Billy, and rut for him like a bitch in heat. She blushed as the urge bubbled up and fought it down again.

The sex had been magnificent, and probably the *were-wolf disease*—she jerked from the words and thought, *rather strange condition*—was contributing to these feelings. She had to keep her head. She had to figure this out.

Aria pulled up to the house, which had a rather beautiful view (weren't most views in Big Sur beautiful?) of the Pacific not half a mile away. That night it was too dark to see the view, though, and she had slipped into the house quietly. She could smell, actually smell, that her roommates were asleep, could hear their regular breathing. Angela was asleep on the couch. Brittany was in her room snoring softly. Kylie likewise, snoring less softly. They had eaten Mexican for dinner, and it lingered like a fog in the common area.

Aria went to her room on tiptoe and closed the door behind her, locking it. She wanted a shower, and she was suddenly powerfully hungry, but she had fallen down in bed, and no more did she rise that night.

She dreamed of a bogglingly flat land with sparse dead grey grass waving in the wind. In the distance was a two-story farmhouse under a boiling sky the color of spoiled milk, and the house filled her with unreasoning terror. Crows circled high above and called down to her in the tongue of crows a warning over and over; beware, beware, beware, beware! The farmhouse door was open (Had it always been? Had it opened just now?), and two glimmering eyes looked out on her with pitiless malice. The wind whistled and howled, and the sound of old boards groaning, ominous and forlorn, made her lie low, belly down in the grass, rooted to the spot in fear and dread of she knew not what. The eyes did not blink, did not waver, but watched her from the darkness of the house.

Something in the basement. She knew there was something bad in the basement but did not know how she knew. She trembled and put her face against the cold clods as the wind howled and stirred the dead grass around her. "Go away," she whispered. *Something in the basement.* "No," she said, louder. *Something bad.* "NO," she said, looking up, jerking her face away, then toward the house. The eyes were gone. The door yawned like a black maw, and she was walking toward it, but she did not want to. *Something in the basement with teeth.* She was climbing the porch stairs. Some part of her was screaming, but she saw herself walking as if asleep, walking forward, her feet bare, her body in a thin white cotton dress of the sort her mother used to put her in when she was small.

She was walking through the door and into shadow, then down a dark hallway that smelled of varnish, and old dust, and something else beneath, something old and sinister. She saw herself opening the door to the basement, a deeper darkness in a house of shadows yielding before her, and with all her will and terror tried to pull away as she descended. There were sounds down there... ripping, rending, screaming, dying sounds... When she reached the bottom of the stairs, a wolfish mask of her own face, bloody and rotting, stared back at her with luminous silver eyes and said in a nightmare growl, "*Eat.*" She awoke screaming and covered in someone else's blood.

CHAPTER 28:
THE HUTCHINS KILLINGS

"The game you seek to learn is layered like an onion. Peel off a strip and another awaits you. And another, and another. The man who seeks to find the secret heart of an onion, gentlemen, is a man who will be bitterly disappointed."
–*Vertical Run*, Joseph Garber

Excerpted from the Introduction of Billy Hatfield's first book, *The Hutchins Killings*:

The bizarre string of murders centered in and around the little town of Hutchins, Nebraska has gone unsolved, although rumors have persisted for almost a century about who (or *what*) committed them. This book means to shed light on what has heretofore been relegated only to legend and to suggest a possible suspect for these brutal killings—killings so brutal, in fact, that few in the little Nebraska town were willing to believe they could have been perpetrated by a human being.

Others who have investigated these crimes in depth have lost themselves for a time, as people of reason will, trying to understand and to make sense of things as senseless and incomprehensible as these events. My own conclusion, after almost five years of interviews and libraries and archives and photographs and moldering onion-skinned police reports, is simply this: we can't put a *why* to events like the ones this book recounts, nor to the myriad of other atrocities carried out by monsters wearing human faces in the 20th century, from Hitler's Final Solution at Auschwitz to the Killing Fields of Cambodia, but perhaps it serves the human animal (who must, after all, put down the world in the shape of a story) if we can inscribe a *who* in the hole of the story where no *who* was before, but in the place where he always belonged.

Excerpted from Chapter I of *The Hutchins Killings*:

Sarah Cady, age 34, was murdered in her bed sometime before dawn, probably about 5am, on January 24th 1921 on the outskirts of North Hutchins, Nebraska. North Hutchins itself, population 559 souls in 1921, was merely a waving strand of wheat fields, cornfields, and dairy farms about ten miles from the main intersection the maps call Hutchins and the locals simply called "town." Hutchins itself boasted 2,000 people and ten municipal employees.

Mrs. Cady's throat was ripped out, and it was never found at the scene or elsewhere. Her heart was pulled explosively from her ribcage, painting the walls. Her liver and kidneys appeared to have been savaged so severely it was unclear whether or not she had been savaged by a madman's blade or by the ravages of some animal's jaws—the damage was too extensive and the coroner, John D. Macy, whose usual fare was at its most outré when some unwary farmer met his end at the wrong end of a harrow or an augur, was simply not up to the task of performing the sort of autopsy one might come to expect today in similar circumstances.

Downstairs, her husband Clive had been awake for about an hour and had just come in from milking the cows, when he says he heard a short but awful scream and a ripping sound like a length of fabric or wet leather being torn slowly by hand. When he got upstairs, the window was open, curtains flapping fecklessly in the icy chill of a predawn breeze in the Nebraska winter. The room looked, one deputy would later remark, as if it had been repainted in shades of darkening red. Much is unknown about the disposition of her body when Clive Cady opened the door to his bedroom and discovered her, both because of his own shock and the delay.

Clive's nearest neighbor, Myron Bellvue, was a mile away through the snowy East Field of the Cady Farm (See Fig. 3). From there, they took Bellvue's truck into town and got the Sheriff, Mr. Hap Verlander by name. They returned in convoy by 0745 where Verlander began his investigation. Coroner Macy did not arrive until 2pm, as his affairs had kept him in North Platte all morning.

Clive claimed never to have seen anything or anyone coming or going on his land that night. He swore that they were not a couple given to quarrelling and had never had a cross word in fifteen years of marriage. He was considered to be a decent and honest man by his neighbors, and none of those who knew them could honestly report they had ever had trouble or heard of it from the Cadys. There had been some mourning in the household about a miscarriage that winter, Sarah's third, but there was never any reason to speculate this was the source of anything but sorrow among other sorrows in the hard life of the childless Nebraska farmer and his wife.

Sarah Cady was interred at the Old Hutchins Cemetery on Route 3404 four days later. Clive, when he went into the ground beside her in 1971, had lived alone as a bachelor in the downstairs bedroom of the farmhouse. The story goes that he refused to climb the stairs of that house from the day she died unto his dying day.

No murder weapon was ever found. No suspect beyond Clive himself (and that was quickly dismissed) were ever seriously questioned. Until now, no one had any evidence to put forward that might bring justice to Sarah Cady's ghost (and many others besides, as those bitter years marched on). My research has uncovered what I believe to be positive proof identifying the man who murdered Sarah Cady that winter morning in 1921.

Excerpted from Chapter V of *The Hutchins Killings*:

One dark night in March of 1905, a baby boy of perhaps ten days in age was discovered squalling on the steps of the Hutchins Courthouse with a tag tied to his finger that said "Lorne Hutchins." Without any official policy to speak of, the Sheriff at the time, Herbert A. Steele, intended to deliver the newborn to the nearest larger town where an orphanage might take him in. (In the interest of posterity, this was very likely not out of apathy or cruelty; Steele was apparently a father of seven children, and there was probably already not enough to go around at the Steele house.) That, perhaps, is when Fate intervened.

Records indicate the child was adopted by a stranger to the town of Hutchins who had just bought a spread far "out there." The records that remain suggest it was an old sodbuster's homestead that had been abandoned since the family died of disease (possibly influenza) some thirty years before. This stranger signed his name Santiago Vega.

This man, I have discovered, was in fact a sadistic murderer who had fled New Orleans after murdering the Madame of a house of ill repute called *The Petite Morte* and burning that brothel to the ground in 1834. One means of identification I have used is an arrest record many years before in Louisiana that identified his scar: a pale scar from ear to ear where an early rival had tried to cut Santiago's throat, and the stitching above and below this line were clearly visible. In his journal, Sheriff Steele mentions this scar on the old man's throat. By the date of the adoption, Santiago Vega was in his

70s, and his reasons to adopt are as dark as the history of what followed.

Lorne Hutchins attended the one-room schoolhouse infrequently, but apparently every time he did, he hurt another child in some terrible way until he was expelled at the age of thirteen, though the official reasons why are lost to history.

Santiago Vega was clearly, according to the school-marm's diaries, beating young Lorne savagely and regularly, and that violence gave way to other violence. If anyone were to so much as whisper of the boy's bruises, he was apt not to tussle with the offending whisperer so much as wait until no one was looking and push the object of his rage off a hilltop or cliff. The schoolmarm suspected him of removing another child's eye once but could not prove it, and none of the children would swear to it. However, wherever "accident" or "misfortune" was, so was Lorne there, if only circling in the back of the crowd.

Santiago Vega died under mysterious circumstances, probably in the autumn of 1920. It was never officially reported, and no death certificate exists. Apparently, however, Lorne remarked to one of the townsfolk, the grocer Gary Hermann, that Vega had been killed by a wolf. "But the wolf," he said, "well, that old wolf, he only *scratched* me before I *kilt him*." Hermann was convinced before this encounter that Lorne was "crazy as a bed-bug" (see Appendix C for excerpts of Hermann's journal) and even more so when the young man pulled up his arm to show him the scar, but no scar existed there.

Lorne Hutchins then, as a boy, had been systematically and cruelly abused by Vega for reasons this author cannot fathom, and I believe this treatment turned the man into a serial killer who often crept into the houses of his distant neighbors and, with nearly inhuman rage, committed unspeakable acts of violence against the men, women, and children of Hutchins, Nebraska in 1921.

CHAPTER 29

IN WHICH ARIA SINGS

Wednesday Morning
May 25, 2016

Aria stood naked in the tree line, covered in blood and with a scream welling up in her throat when she heard a voice, warm and gentle behind her, "Easy there, girl. Breathe."

She turned and standing there was a man in a dark coat with short dark hair and piercing brown eyes.

"My name is Father Giovanni Santa Ana," he said, his voice gentle and reassuring. He offered her his coat. "You look like you could use some help."

She trembled, cold in the pale mists of dawn, and slipped into his coat. "Th-th-thank you," she said, but her voice was raw, and her throat felt ravaged. Her skin was thick with drying, tacky blood as bright as red paint.

"Wh-what happened? Why am I…?"

"Yes," said Father Giovanni, sympathy in his eyes. "I'm afraid you don't want to go back inside."

"M-my roommates—" she began, then stopped. Her panic was beginning to betray itself in her voice as the fog cleared. *Had she? Oh God no, please.*

"Your roommates are with Our Lord, Aria," he said gently. "I'm sorry."

Her legs felt funny, and her head felt like little bubbles were floating up from her brainstem and popping in the middle of her forehead. She had time to think *panic attack* and then she was on the ground.

"Do not be afraid," he said. "I'll take care of you."

When she awakened hours later, she was in a cot under a gently flapping tent ceiling. For a time, she could not place where she was or what happened, but in a moment, she remembered and, swallowing the horror, she rose. Aria found she had been washed of the blood and was wearing her own clothes—panties, sports bra, t-shirt, jeans, socks. Her hiking boots sitting outside the tent-flap neatly atop a small tarp. A fire crackled nearby, and the sizzle of meat made her salivate. The smell of wood smoke and cooking meat beneath it seemed to blot out the waking nightmare—for a moment—of what she had done and what she had become. The priest was seated on a log in front of the fire, turning sausage in a small aluminum pan.

"Breakfast," he said as she stepped out, gesturing to a blue metal plate splotched with white on the opposite log. They were in a stand of trees in the highlands a few miles inland from where she had lost consciousness.

"You carried me here?"

"This is my camp," he said. "And we can talk here."

"Talk about what?" she asked. "Who are you? Why are you… uh… I mean, it's not normal for someone to find a bloody, screaming woman and some murdered girls and act like it's just Wednesday… and then to carry someone you just met, unconscious, through rough country for miles and then to wash and dress her from clothes you took from her house… *Who are you?*"

He smiled softly, "That's a lot of questions before breakfast." He lifted the pan and offered the sausage. She took some on her plate and sat.

"Coffee?" he asked.

She nodded, and he produced a percolator, poured into a blue tin cup, and handed it to her, "No cream or sugar, sorry."

"It's fine," she said and began to eat more hungrily than she might have believed.

When she had finished and helped herself to seconds, Giovanni said, "Aria, tell me how this happened. I noticed those burns on your fingers when I was dressing you (and forgive me for taking the liberty, but it seemed best to carry a clothed, unconscious girl than a naked one, should we meet other travelers). How were you burned?"

"I. Um. Wait, no, first you answer my questions."

"Right," he said. "Fair enough. Let's see… I work for the Mother Church. I am part of a Holy Order that has vowed to combat works of supernatural evil in the world on behalf of Our Lord. It is my business to see things like I saw this morning and to learn the truth of what has happened and to take action when sanctioned by the Church."

"You're an Inquisitor," she said softly, with dawning horror.

"I suppose you could put it that way," he said.

"And you're here to kill me or exorcise me or something?"

"No," he said. "I would rather not kill you and I am not usually the one they call in for exorcism."

"Well," she said, "then what are you here for?"

"I'd like to know who brought the disease here," he said, spreading his hands, "and I would like to protect as many people as possible from monsters. I want to save lives."

"Well," she said, "I... so, what do you want from me?"

"I'd like you to tell me what happened," he said with quiet patience.

She considered this for a moment, and then she did tell him. When she had finished, he nodded.

"Thank you," he said evenly, "Perhaps we can go together and talk to this Mr. Hatfield, and he can tell us what happened to him, and in this way, we can trace it back to a source. Will you go with me and make the introductions, please, Aria?"

"Yes," she said, "if it helps save lives."

"God willing, it shall," he said.

But doubts battened on her like hungry ghosts. "What about my house? My friends? We can't just leave them there," she said.

"I took the liberty of calling in a crew to help from your landline," he said.

"A crew?"

"Sometimes when incidents like these take place, it is in the best interest of the community if a more palatable explanation is offered. The Church sometimes involves itself in an unofficial capacity to this end. Crews are sometimes dispatched to scrub an area where something unfortunate, like this morning's unpleasantness, has taken place. Until the disease is contained and all the infected are identified and advised of their responsibilities, it is necessary to control how much the authorities may come to know. Your friends will probably be reputed to have driven off a cliff in the early hours of this morning, and their bodies are likely to be lost to the sea. This is more merciful for their families than the truth or a disappearance that will damn them to a lifetime of uncertainty and unfulfilled hope, wouldn't you agree?"

She recoiled at the smoothness of it, the calm rationality of it, the masonry of rationalization that justified... well... anything. Anything at all, and yet she could not refute it. That was the special hell of it. She could not gainsay what Father Giovanni had said with anything more than anger in search of an argument.

"Yes," she said quietly after a moment.

"Good," he said. "After we strike camp, let us go and talk to your lover, the prolific Mr. Hatfield. The crew will do its work, and we should be about ours."

CHAPTER 30:

THE VIOLENT DEMISE OF SANTIAGO VEGA

Dusk
October 31, 1920

B ent and gray, now over a century old, the cracked and wrinkled face of Santiago Vega looked out on the rising darkness over the forlorn and empty corn- fields from the farmhouse kitchen with strange unease and limped to the cellar door. He jerked it open and peered down into the dark. A fetid smell of shit and body odor rose out of the cellar.

"Get up here," he called, his voice the croak of a carrion bird, low with age and dull loathing.

The boy, filthy, bone-skinny and in one filthy rag climbed the stairs quickly. His eyes dark with circles and quick with hunger and thirst.

"That'll teach you to overcook my eggs, maggot," he said, quietly into the boy's ear as he passed by. "Now you've got chores to do, then you can wash, and then I want supper, and if you fuck it up, another *week* in the *dark* for you."

Lorne said nothing and set about his "chores," which were a litany of tasks that ranged from the trivial sundries of the household to work around the farm that the old man had grown too lazy or arthritic to do. Lorne wondered, sometimes, down in the dark if he couldn't kill Santiago. Take a shovel to his skull in the night, or push him down the cellar stairs, or bury the sickle they used to harrow the fields in the old man's chest, but he couldn't. He hated the old man, but even in his dreams he knew that to raise a hand against him would mean failure first, and afterward, terrible pain. Still, it was a thought that recurred often. Perhaps... perhaps one day...

The sun was just about down. Lorne went out and drew water from the hand pump for supper, washing his hands and face in the process. Then he stiffened and looked around, shivering in the chill of the autumn evening. He felt, was sure as animals are sure, that he was being watched. Lorne looked around, saw nothing, heard nothing, and felt a shiver that had little to do with the cold slide like bony fingers of ice up his back.

He shivered, then it passed, and he picked up his bucket. He carried the bucket carefully into the house, aware of the hiding he would take if he spilled even a drop on the floor, then fired the stove and began to prepare their supper. If it was dry or undercooked, he could expect to live days in the dark, coming up only to do what tasks Santiago set him before being banished again to the darkness under the house. He dreamed of leaving, but he had tried that once; Santiago had found him on the road and beaten him to within an inch of his life. Escape, next time, would either be successful or fatal.

Lorne prepared the meal while Santiago limped to his bedroom. The old man was secretive, paranoid, and full of strange fancies. For many years, Lorne had not understood it, but recently he had begun to wonder if Santiago was not afraid, afraid in his bones, of something. He kept a shotgun ready, and his cane had a blade in it. In his better moods, if he had drunk a fair bit of wine, Santiago would tell Lorne of the many men he had killed in his life, of the towns he had visited, of cardrooms and cat-houses and fortunes he had made and lost in his time as a grifter and a gambler. He was fond of saying he had never allowed an insult to go unanswered in his life in these rare storytelling moments.

Lorne, who had never been farther than Hutchins in his young life (and there only a handful of times), was somewhat in awe of Santiago's travels and experiences. He loved the idea of taking to the road, drifting, beholden to no one but your own belly when it growled.

They ate at the scored and rickety dining room table in silence. Lorne watched the old man eat intensely, searching his face for disapproval of the slightest thing, knowing it would mean blood and pain for himself, unaware of just how much stronger he was than the old man if he only dared. Suddenly, a rock came hurtling through the kitchen window. The old man roared out a curse as the stone connected with the back of his head, knocking him to the ground as glass flew across the room.

Lorne stood up, watching the blood pour from the old man's head, unsure what to do. The door burst open behind him, and an ancient wolfman, hair patchy and gray, eyes milky and pale, stepped in with a stertorous snarl. The boy stepped back, back all the way to the wall, slowly, his eyes as wide as train tunnels.

The wolf pawed forward on all fours, coughing and growling low in his throat, "I found you, Vega. Found you at last…"

The old man moaned, rolled over, and his eyes met the wolf's.

"No," he said. "No, noooooo."

"For Bethany, yes… *oh yes*," said the wolf, looming now over Santiago, opening his jaws impossibly wide, and splintering the old man's skull like kindling at the precise moment a shotgun slug ripped through his spine and opened a dinner-plate sized hole in his chest. The beast howled in rage and turned to see Lorne with a shotgun by the front door, a trickle of urine running down his leg.

The wolf staggered, then moaned, bleeding buckets on the floor in hot arterial gushes. The ancient monster leaped at the boy. Lorne squeezed the trigger and the other half of the beast's chest disappeared, but its momentum carried it forward and on top of him, scratching and pawing him as they both tumbled to the ground, and then it lay still.

Silence.

Lorne lay still for a long time, and when he looked down it wasn't a wolf creature before him, but a withered old man, older, perhaps than even Santiago Vega had been before his timely end.

He rolled the stiffening corpse off of him. He checked for anything broken and found none—just cuts and bruises. The creature had scratched him deeply up the arm in its death throes, but Lorne concluded he was going to be fine. He walked over to Vega stared down at the old man's ruined corpse on the bloody floor with burning hatred in his soul hot enough to raise the temperature in Hell. And he smiled.

He buried them in the cornfield at first light. After they were in the ground, the boy stood in the cold light on that desolate flatland and looked west. He considered the cobweb-thin ribbons of last night's dreams, a wolf, terrible hunger, and he wished bitterly he had been the one to kill Santiago. He would have to visit his hatred on other men. Oh yes, he would.

He turned from the unmarked graves and walked back toward the farmhouse with murder on his mind. And wolves.

CHAPTER 31

FRANK CONNECTS THE DOTS AND BILLY HAS A VISITOR

Noon
Wednesday
May 25, 2016

S eated alone at a table in the near-empty Big Sur Public Library, Frank put down the library's copy of *The Hutchins Killings* and whistled appreciatively. This Billy Hatfield had done some pretty fair detective work to finger this Lorne Hutchins kid for the murders in Nebraska, and some of those crime scenes in the book were eerily familiar to scenes Frank had visited. Impressive. But the book wasn't able to track what had ever happened to Lorne. The old farmhouse was empty and fallen in long ago, the book said, with no real clues as to when it had been abandoned but probably some-time in the mid-1920s.

Lela came over to him and put a hand on his shoulder. "So? What do you think?"

"I'd like a word with him. Mind if I use your phone?"

"Official police business, detective?" she said officiously.

"You know it, Miss Lady" he said.

"Then, I suppose so."

Andy picked up on the fourth ring. "Go."

"Can you run a name for me?"

"Shoot."

"Lorne Hutchins, DOB is on or about 1905, out of Nebraska."

"Sure," said Andy. "Why?"

"Just wondering what we have on him. Also, what have you found?"

"Teams have been looking for likely sites. So far, nothing, but we're still looking. Also, it turns out Billy Hatfield is renting a cabin out near Lime Creek off Dolan Ridge for the summer. Got an address for you if you're ready."

Frank took down the address and said, "Thanks. I'm heading over to Hatfield's, then. I'll call you later."

"Right," said Andy, "You want some backup? Is this a suspect?"

"I'm not sure what he is, but right now he's in the right place at the wrong time, and I'm curious enough to go talk to him. Ask him why his Caddie was parked in front of Fernwood all weekend. You can come along if you like."

"I'll meet you there," said Andy, and hung up.

The driveway was rough and potholed and led meanderingly into the clearing where the cabin stood. Father Giovanni and Aria drove up in her car. She parked and got out.

"Billy?" she called, climbing the stairs. The door opened, and Billy's face smiled to her in greeting then looked at the man behind her, and a cloud passed over his face.

"Hi," he said. "I thought you'd be back sooner. Are you okay?"

She folded herself in his arms, breathing him in, and tried not to sob when she thought of what had happened. She held her breath until the threatening sobs retreated. She wiped her eyes on her sleeves.

"Hey? What's up? Are you okay?" he asked, hugging her.

"I'm fine," she said. "This is Father Giovanni Santa Ana. He's, uh... here to talk to you."

"Pleased to meet you, Mr. Hatfield. I admire your work," said the priest, holding out his hand to shake.

Billy did not take his hand but rather said "How can I help you, Father?"

"I wondered if we might have a word about your recent experiences, Mr. Hatfield," said the priest.

"Where's Nob?" asked Aria.

"Left after breakfast," said Billy. "Said he wanted to look a few things up. And sure, Father, come in."

They stepped inside. Billy read fear and distress in Aria's eyes, but the priest seemed benignly polite. He wondered for a moment if the man could be dangerous to them then dismissed the idea.

The priest sat down in a chair and said, "I'll speak plainly, Mr. Hatfield, if you'll forgive me for what may come off as bluntness, but I believe we have little time to waste."

"By all means," said Billy, "let's have it."

"You wrote about a man named Lorne Hutchins and about the murders he carried out in the winter of 1921. The Church has files on this man because he was something more than a serial killer and a cannibal; he was a werewolf. Werewolves, I am afraid, have a very long lifespan—there have been cases of the strongest of them living for centuries, while others weaken after about a hundred years, some may go on, appearing to age very slowly. Hutchins dropped out of sight after an incident in Chambers, Arizona in 1947. He probably has more murders under his belt than any other werewolf in history we are aware of, if I had to guess, many of which we will never know about. I believe he is probably still alive. After all, he was only 15 years old when he was infected in October of 1920. It is therefore more than a coincidence to my mind that you, who wrote a book about him (of which he is undoubtedly aware, I fear), have encountered the werewolf's curse, and even passed it along to Miss Davis here in very short order."

Billy wanted to protest, felt his gorge rising and his face flushing as if stabbed by hundreds of pink needles, but he could say nothing. Fear was humming and buzzing inside him like a hive of furious wasps. He opened his mouth and shut it again. Twice.

"I have come to discuss the situation with you, and more importantly, to learn how you were infected."

"I don't want to talk about that," said Billy. "I can't talk about that."

"I'm afraid it may be your only hope," said Father Giovanni gently, "because there is a demon in your blood now, and it wants you to do unspeakable things— some of which you have already given in to and others which you do not yet dream, but that will bear bitter fruit in the fullness of time. These things you will do are poison to the soul, degenerative to the character, and infectious to the community. In a century of such acts, no trace will remain of the good man I believe you are today. I ask you again, how did you contract this moon-driven wolf-sickness sometimes called The Diana Strain?"

"I was sure it was a dream," Billy said pleadingly, "I was *sure* it was *only a dream*! Don't you see? Don't you *see?*" He was beginning to itch with long, rough hair beneath the flesh of his arms and legs, his voice box felt tight, his fingernails felt pulled at the cuticle.

Father Giovanni rose. "It's all right," he said. "Calm down. I see. I understand. Relax. Breathe. Push it away, Mr. Hatfield."

Aria felt the Change rising in her in response to Billy's change. She fought it back down as a wave of nausea passed over her and went to Billy, whispering and soothing him, caressing him.

"Perhaps some water?" said the priest.

Billy nodded. Father Giovanni stepped into the kitchen, opened the refrigerator, and returned with two bottles of water he found there.

Billy and Aria both drank, and no one spoke for a long time. Finally they sat down, and the priest sat down across from them.

"Tell me what happened, please, Billy," said Father Giovanni softly.

Billy sighed, then stood, and began pacing back and forth as he spoke, looking at the floor, the walls, but never at Aria or Giovanni.

"It was my first night here. I can't explain why I had to come to Big Sur, exactly, but it was hard to write at my place in the hills. I needed water. I've been working on a novel, but it wasn't going anywhere. I thought maybe a change of scenery would help, but why I chose this place I'm not sure, in fact, I'm less sure than ever. I was having a lot of dreams about some of what I had researched in Nebraska, about the Hutchins killings. I'd gone out there, of course, when I was writing that book and walked over the ground. I talked to Old Timers who remembered things. It got in my head, and I had nightmares for a long time. I wasn't exactly afraid, just horrified by the murders—the blind hatred inside them.

So, I came and rented a cabin. That first night the writing was good. I got a few thousand words down and went to bed. I thought I dreamed that sometime in the night, *he* came in. He came in so quietly that I was sure I was dreaming. No man can be so silent and pass through space. He was grizzled, but I knew his face; it was Hutchins. Hutchins in his late forties or early fifties, as he would have been decades ago, but I knew the face from pictures I'd discovered from school records, class photographs, and the like. He came to me and said I would suffer for writing about him. I couldn't move, I couldn't speak, I was afraid, but it was something else. I felt heavy and drugged and full of sleep. He produced a needle and stuck in in my arm—I slept.

I woke up on the floor late in the morning with a terrible taste in my mouth and little cuts on my chest and arms. I figured I'd done it to myself during the nightmare. I figured it was all just work getting to me. That happens to writers, you know? I never thought for a second that he could, or would, ever find me. But he was *here*," said Billy with a shiver. "He was *in this house*."

Father Giovanni nodded, as if his suspicions had been totally confirmed.

"It's strange that he drew you here," said the priest, "I've never heard of that happening before. Interesting."

"So, now what?" asked Billy, "I told you my story. You said it was my last hope. Where's the hope?"

"It is here," said the priest, and he shot Billy in the head.

Billy fell, the wood baseboards red and gray with brains and blood and white with chips of bone. Aria screamed, then ripped out of her own skin and into wolf form, roaring in rage and pain.

She swiped at him, running in blind berserk fury, but Giovanni rolled to the side, picked up the coffee table and hurled it at her, drew a bead and fired, but the shot went wide as she juked left then ran along the side of the wall, agile and fast.

Suddenly there was a car racing up the driveway and the sound of running feet.

Frank and Andy burst through the door with guns drawn, made dynamic entry into the room, screaming at Father Giovanni to drop the revolver, and the she-wolf darted down the hall and crashed out the back window.

Both of the lawmen saw her at the same moment, and their jaws dropped open.

"Ho-ly sh—" said Frank.

Father Giovanni dropped the pistol and said calmly, "I surrender, gentlemen."

CHAPTER 32:

GOOD EATS

Chambers, Arizona
Summer
1947

It was a boxcar diner on Route 66 with a neon sign in red and white that said *Good Eats*. Lorne Hutchins had come to possess it a decade earlier and had operated it since then. What happened in the intervening years between Hutchins and Chambers is lost to time, but what is known to the *Gladius Dei* is that he murdered an estimated two hundred motorists and truckers and disposed of their bodies by serving them to his customers or consuming them himself. The Order got wind of this in large part because of well-placed informants within the FBI, who had traced a number of disappearances to this particular stretch of Route 66 and had begun a surreptitious investigation in the winter of 1946.

The night the diner burned began as most others did for Lorne. Earlier in the week, he had killed a lone motorist (he almost never took more than one at a time, and almost never in the diner itself, nor ever in daylight, nor ever too far to carry the body back to the diner). He was in the freezer for an hour after the work of butchering, which he did in a small shed outside the diner. The shed was fitted with a tiled floor and a large drain in the center of it, and hooks suspended from the reinforced ceiling. He also purchased hogs and cattle from the slaughterhouse and sometimes they hung right alongside unwary, unlucky traveling salesmen whose travels had come to an end. Lorne thought this a great joke and laughed often to see it. Men, he decided, hung just as well from a meat hook as any hog ever slit open at the throat had. Often the homemade sausages at *Good Eats* got high praise from his customers, even (and this he relished above all good jokes) the Arizona State Troopers assigned to this stretch of road.

At first it had been a problem disposing of vehicles after their owners had ceased to require their use, but Lorne had discovered a deep and abandoned silver mine at the base of the ridge a few miles away, and since then he had no trouble, but it was a night's work after all to decide a target was alone after dark, wait until the place was empty, catch up with him by stealth or guile, kill him quietly and neatly (Lorne had learned the trick of breaking the neck with his thickly corded wolf-arms and spilling no blood at all. He could do it in seconds), then carry the body back, stow it in the shed, then drive the dead man's car to the old mine, dump it, and run back as a wolf to butcher the body before first light. Still, Lorne was energetic, and motivated by seething malice like a fever behind his eyes.

The day had been hot, around 114 degrees at noon, and it was still in the 90s as the Arizona sun was going down over the desert. Agent Paul McSweeney pulled into the dusty gravel parking lot of *Good Eats* and peered inside. He and two other agents had been watching the diner for about six months with very little to show for it. Hutchins seemed to be able to tell when he was being watched and was cautious in the extreme. He lived in a small house behind the diner but spent almost no time there. Indeed, it had become a joke during the investigation that you'd have to wake up pretty early in the morning to catch some crooks, but how do you catch a guy who never seems to sleep?

Agent McSweeney idly reviewed the sheet with the man's description again, as he had for weeks. He could recite it from memory, and yet the old ritual held some kind of meditative power as the minutes ticked by: six feet two inches, one hundred and ninety pounds, scars across his chest, arms, and back consistent with the scoring of a whip, blonde hair cropped close, blue eyes, light stubble, pale complexion, and extremely white teeth with rather pronounced canines.

This was their prey. This was the subject of the Bureau's attention. This is where the trail of travelers had ended, but so far they had found no evidence, caught no scent of this being anything more than an ordinary diner in the middle of the desert on "The Main Street of America," with an extremely energetic, if somewhat mysterious, proprietor.

McSweeney watched the front door, and right on time, his partner, John Sherman by name, pulled up in a dusty Mercury, climbed out, and walked into the diner. They had decided, at long last, to send someone in. Two someones, as it happened. McSweeney took a deep breath, stashed the description sheet in the glove box of the Ford, then locked the doors and sauntered in—a full two minutes after Sherman had gone in and sat down at the counter.

The big man on the grill turned, regarding them both with cool eyes, "What can I get you, mister?"

"Draw one in the dark for me, Mac," said McSweeney, sitting down at a booth toward the rear of the diner.

"And you?" Hutchins asked Sherman, pouring McSweeney's coffee and coming around the counter to place it in front of him at the bar.

Hutchins' shoulders and arms were powerful-looking, his back broad and thick—but he moved easily, gracefully, and rather quietly for a man his size. McSweeney decided then if it came to a fight, he'd just shoot the son of a bitch, because two men probably wouldn't be enough to best him if Hutchins decided to fight. He appreciated the weight of his pistol in its leather shoulder-holster.

"You got specials today?" asked Sherman over his shoulder, tracking Hutchins.

"Pork Chops," said Hutchins with a strange smile, "and mashed taters with gravy."

"Sounds good," said Sherman. "I'll have that."

Hutchins nodded and got on the grill, eyeing the mirror he had under the hood periodically so he could watch the room and the parking lot beyond.

A few moments passed in silence but for the sizzle of meat on the grill, then Lorne ladled out a slab of steaming mashed potatoes and poured a generous helping of thick, brown gravy from a simmering pan, lay two golden pork chops on the loaded plate with carrots and set it down in front of Agent Sherman, but instead of moving away, he stood there stock still and silent.

"Eat," he said in what was almost a friendly voice.

Sherman looked down, picked up his knife and fork, and began to eat, his eyes thereafter never leaving Hutchins' own glacier cool eyes.

"Tasty," said Sherman. And he thought it was. The pork chops were remarkably supple and moist.

Hutchins nodded, then after a moment of watching Sherman eat, he said, "I'm pleased to hear you say that." He leaned forward conspiratorially and said, "You know, my Pa used to whip me but good if I burned dinner. I guess you'd think, wouldn't you, that I'd hate him for that. Yeah, took a bullwhip to me, flayed flesh from bone sometimes. Taught me a lot, my Pa. Taught me a lot about life. Hell, I thank him. I thank him for teaching me. He taught me to read, even, and to write. To read books. You do much reading, Mister?"

"No," said John Sherman, nearly nose to nose with Lorne.

"I liked to read about the old stories. The old ways. Like, that old Greek story, Lycaon. Ever hear that story?"

Sherman shook his head, trying to decide if Hutchins had made him and knew him for a G-Man, or if he was just being conversational—there was something unsettling in the man's solicitousness and the drift of the conversation.

"Well, I'll tell you the story," said Hutchins, "There was a mean old coot of a King name of Lycaon, and he was all bad and extra rattlesnake mean in a time when ordinary folks were just *real bad*. And it got so people told stories about things he'd done, and soon enough Zeus (that's the Pa of the gods back then before Jesus' Daddy), he comes down to see what's what, right? See if this Lycaon is as bad as the people are saying. Zeus can huck lightning bolts and call down curses as bad as you like, see? And he comes in power into that King's Court and everybody's on his knees pleading and crying for mercy that he won't take a lightning-whip to their backsides, all of 'em that is, except bad old King Lycaon who says he doesn't even much believe this man before him is a god, much less the Daddy of all gods. And he tells Zeus he'd best submit to a test. Zeus, well, he just fixes old Lycaon with a grin and says he'll go along sure as sure. 'Test away,' he says.

"Well, bad old King Lycaon calls for a big banquet, orders the whole spread put out—all the wine and grits and squash and greens and fatback, it all goes to the table for the feast. He goes back into the kitchen, and he fixes a special plate for the one he thinks isn't Zeus, and comes back with a dead messenger baked in a pie. Puts it in front of him and says, 'Eat up.' Well, Zeus knows shit from shinola, and he stands up and calls down a curse special for King Lycaon right on the spot, turns him into a wolf with a man's eyes. 'If you can hold back from tasting human flesh for nine years,' says Zeus, 'I reckon you can wear a man's skin again, but otherwise you'll be bound forever as you are until you die and go to Hell.' Then he turned that old King's castle into a shrine to himself, as a reminder to every Tom, Dick, or Harry who passed that way of what had happened there and what Zeus could do in revenge if he wanted it. Now, you ever heard that story, hoss?"

"No," said Sherman, his face white, his eyes wide, "I never have."

"Feller name of Pausanias set it down in 480 B.C. or so. My Pa taught me that story and learned me to read it. Do you know why?"

"No. Why?" asked Sherman, his mouth dry.

"Because Pa meant for me to know three somethings about this old world. You stand your ground even if a god who can huck lightning comes to your door and everybody else goes weak in the knees, for one. Two: if you do something mean and bad enough to offend Heaven, at least you got their attention, and lastest and mostest... you may get yourself cursed, but if that curse is teeth and appetite, you'd best just go on ahead and eat." He smiled a ghastly, unpleasant smile and there was a burning, seething madness in his eyes that made Sherman, who had faced down gangsters from Brooklyn to Chicago in the course of his duties as a lawman, draw back in shrinking fear.

Then, without prelude or warning, a collared priest came through the door and out of the gloom of dusk with a double-barreled shotgun on his hip, levelled it at Hutchins and fired. Glasses and ketchup bottles and carafes of water exploded along with the mirror on the back wall above the grill.

Hutchins dove behind the counter. Both agents drew their Colt 1911 .45s and hit the deck, levelling their pistols at the priest, but the snarl from the other side of the long counter froze the very blood in their veins with its savage intensity.

The priest, an athletic-looking man in his 30s with an Irish face and shocking red hair, snapped the shotgun open at the breach, dropped two shells, loaded two more, and leaned over the counter and fired another shot in the general direction of the growl.

"You'll all die tonight," came a hideous, bass roar that seemed to shake the very floorboards of the boxcar.

Then, a flaming rag knotted in the neck to a bottle of whiskey came whistling end over end and exploded against the priest's skull; even as he was consumed in flame and began to scream, a dark shape loomed up and up impossibly huge and tawny as the desert itself, a wolf that walked as a man, poured like liquid smoke over the counter and landed squarely on John Sherman, claws tearing at the man's chest, head, and neck viciously.

Paul McSweeney, crouched beside the rear booth squeezed off seven very accurate shots into the creature's head. The shots registered terribly and very loudly in the confined space of the boxcar diner, changing the very pressure of the room, even as the priest at the other end had now become indistinguishable except as a dark shape in the white heat of a wall engulfed in flame—the interior was filling with smoke.

McSweeney reloaded, crawled forward to his partner, whose blood was gushing from his jugular vein in terrible spurts. He slammed a wad of napkins onto the man's neck, eyes watching the motionless wolfman with seven holes in his head as he lay motionless several feet away. Agent McSweeney screamed at John Sherman to stay awake, to apply pressure to his wound, and he lifted his friend, sat him in the adjacent booth, shot and then kicked out the window, and threw his partner, then himself, out of the inferno.

Special Agent John Sherman died an hour later on the way to the hospital. Special Agent Paul McSweeney's report was reviewed at the highest level by the Director himself, then buried. After the commendation for bravery in his attempt to save the life of another agent, he was given a (basement) desk job at Quantico where he was guaranteed to speak to no one.

The only remains ever found in the burned out husk of *Good Eats* was that of a Father Peter O'Malley, formerly of County Meath, assigned to Our Lady of the Immaculate Conception in Tuscon Arizona, and late of the *Gladius Dei*, a name unknown to the Federal Bureau of Investigation until that month and year.

Paul McSweeney retired in 1971 from the Bureau and was fifteen years deceased when Billy Hatfield called his Providence home in the winter of 2010 to ask him about the incident. Paul's wife could provide no information; her only clues had been occasional mutterings in dreams, and things hinted at darkly in the last years when his dementia got, as she put it, "pretty bad."

Whatever Hatfield suspected, McSweeney's experiences never made it into *The Hutchins Killings*, and Billy Hatfield never found in that interview any conclusive proof of whatever happened to Lorne Hutchins.

CHAPTER 33:
FATHER GIOVANNI MAKES CONFESSION

3pm
Wednesday
May 25, 2016

The priest sat composed before the table of the interrogation room of the Sheriff's Office substation in Big Sur. His arms were folded almost in a gesture of prayer when Andy and Frank walked in and sat down across from him.

"You understand you have a right to have an attorney present during questioning?" asked Frank.

"I understand. No need for an attorney, Detective Crow."

"What were you doing at Hatfield's Cabin?" asked Andy.

"I was there to kill him," said the priest, somehow both casually and with the precise and glacial surety found in men of (pardon the pun) conviction.

"Why is that?" asked Frank, "Aren't there rules against that sort of thing in the Church? Thou shalt not...so on and so forth."

"Yes, murder is an abomination before God," said the priest, "but I did not commit murder."

"How do you figure that? Are you denying you shot Billy Hatfield in the head?" asked Frank.

"No," said the priest, "I shot Billy Hatfield in the head and killed him, but it was not murder."

"Why not?" asked Andy.

Father Giovanni looked up with eyes as impassive as winter and said, "The thing in the shape of Billy Hatfield was not a man any longer. He had become a beast. He committed the murders you are investigating, Detective. He was infected with a strain of lycanthropy that originates in Norway before the turn of the last millennium. At the time he did those horrible things, he was not himself, but that made him no less dangerous, both as a vector of infection and as a ravening, murderous animal." He said it all so coolly and with such matter-of-fact certainty that he was almost believable, for a moment.

"Lycanthropy? Is that like, thinking you're a wolf?" asked Frank.

"In this context, it is more than just thinking, Detective," said Father Giovanni.

"You really believe that?" asked Andy.

"Seeing is believing," said Father Giovanni, "Have you seen nothing in recent days that make you wonder in the night if there are, perhaps, stranger things in Heaven and Earth than are dreamed of in your police blotter?"

"Let's go back a bit. How do you know he was a werewolf? For that matter, how did you come to believe such things even exist?" asked Frank.

"I wonder, Detective, if you would do me the kindness of telling me the time," said Father Giovanni.

Frank checked his watch, "I have three o'clock. Why?"

"We should have time for this story, then," said Father Giovanni.

"What do you mean? You think you're going somewhere? There's no bail for Murder One, Father," said Andy.

"I don't need to post bail," said Father Giovanni, "but I will be a free man by dark, all the same."

"How do you figure?" asked Frank.

"Well, let me tell you the story, it may answer several questions at once. You asked me how I came to believe in Lycanthropy. I've come to believe in many things through experience. I met my first werewolf in the French countryside, near an abandoned abbey in Auvergne in 1986. I was young then, only about fifteen years old. That land has a long history with such things. I assume you've heard of La Bete du Gévaudan?"

Andy nodded, but Frank shook his head, "Sorry, not my genre."

"As it was not mine. I couldn't have told you the story as a boy," said Giovanni, "but it amounts to this:

for several years the countryside was terrorized by an enormous wolf that evaded capture with unsettling, almost mystical skill and cunning. Many of the country folk were killed. The King of France even put a bounty on its head, but to no avail for a long time. And then they killed... something. Whatever they brought to the court of the King was a put-up job, to use an Americanism. Some taxidermist's dark fantasy. Rumors persisted that the real Beast was, perhaps, never killed but merely went elsewhere to feed... At any rate, my best friend Remy and I were wandering over France that summer and were in Auvergne that night. We'd secured a room at an Inn in the shadow of the hilltop where the ruined abbey sort of loomed over the village it had probably fostered centuries before. We decided, as it was a moonlit night and we were young fools, to go climb those ruins under the full moon.

"We followed the snaking path up the hill to the tumbled stones of the main gate, and though it was darker inside, under the shadows of those crumbling walls, we went in anyway without so much as a torch (but with a bottle of *vin rouge*) between us. We heard strange noises from within, faint at first, then stronger as we drew closer to the interior. There was a glow of flames inside, a bonfire. We thought it might be young people like ourselves, out for a little fun. It was not. What we saw in the center of the abbey was a convocation of demons.

Witches with black veils and werewolves—or sometimes only men with the heads of wolves—were dancing and chanting and circling and howling, cackling madly.

Some of the wolves were entering the witches, who hiked up skirts or abandoned them entirely and danced under the moon, slathered in the grease of cooked meat, we could smell it broiling over the fire.

Remy and I were shocked at first and not a little drunk, but we did not cry out. Rather, we retreated as quietly as we might, but we did not expect the latecomer to the festivities. A wolf who walked as a man would walk, but larger than any wolf I had ever seen or heard of, came stalking through the arched gateway of the entrance toward us, then threw back its head and howled a full-throated alarm, then leaped in one easy motion, snapped its head to one side as if on some kind of hydraulic spring, and came down with Remy's throat in its jaws. It jerked its massive head with a wet snap, and my friend shivered twice then lay still.

He hadn't even had time to scream, but I screamed. And I wish I could say I had pulled out a knife or picked up a stone and hacked at the monster as it fed on him, but I did not. I could not. I was too surprised, too frightened, too untrained, too *offended* by the very idea that such things could even exist."

The priest looked at both of them and said, "What happened next saved my life, and altered the course of my destiny. A team of three warriors from the Church emerged from the darkness. The wolves called from their dance by the flames inside the abbey came charging out just in time to meet a hail of silver bullets. They moved as one, like a wave entering the abbey, wasting no words and no bullets.

"When they reached me, one of them threw me to the ground and knelt with his knee on my back, and his own to a wall, covering his mates. The wolves retreated, then resurged, sallying forth through forlorn piles of stone. But the riflemen were precise, and conservative of ammunition. They put the beasts down as they came on. Final count was two dozen. The witches who knew the trick vanished… or become as shadows and slipped away, or had flown into the sky, but a few novices remained behind."

"They were taken prisoner and brought back for examination and trial by the Church. I was taken, too, and offered an opportunity to avenge my friend's loss—the French newspapers would say that he had fallen from the walls of the abbey that night, a drunken tragedy and a cautionary tale to other foolish youths. But they asked me if I would care to learn to hunt monsters and to avenge my friend Remy. I accepted.

"I was trained then loaned out to the Polish government. I spent six years with the GROM doing special work in Europe before being accepted for Hunter training in Roma. I have operated since then such as I may, in service to the Church and to God."

There was a long silence. Had they not seen all they had seen, they would dismiss him as a liar or a madman. Only, they had seen that *creature* burst out the back window of Billy Hatfield's cabin. They had seen the knocked-over van that Mira Franklin had been ripped apart and *eaten* in. They had seen the grisly remains of Blake Trezor, the meal made of Ranger John Abrams, and the inhuman strength used to feed on Hunter Shaw and feast upon Madison Blakely. They knew, somehow, that this man had told them the truth as he believed it.

"If there really is such a thing, why doesn't science know about it? And if the Church is secretly hunting monsters, why would you just tell us?" asked Andy.

"The Church certainly has—well, let's not call them 'factions.' Let's call them 'schools of thought' if that tastes better going down. One maintains that people *should* absolutely know about the supernatural evil that walks the Earth. Some believe it would draw many in this secular world back to the Mother Church and to Jesus. Others, however, want to protect people from the truth for their own good—let not their dreams be troubled. Let us, rather, stand guard against the darkness, silently in God's Holy Name, but without burdening our brothers and sisters with the dark knowledge we ourselves have to bear.

"My politics are irrelevant. I'm a soldier. But I tell you about it for a few reasons. I respect you and the work you do. It is not dissimilar to my own in some ways. We are watchmen tending sheep and warding off wolves. Therefore, I want to prepare you for what is to come, so you may survive both professionally and personally."

"What are you talking about?" asked Frank, faint irritation creeping into his voice, "Prepare *us*? You shot a man in the head you claim is a werewolf, you think you'll be out of here by dark, and you're doing *us* a favor by telling us that you're a soldier that kills the things that go bump in the—save it, pal. You're out of your tree."

"Detective," said Father Giovanni gently, patiently, "Very soon, tremendous pressure is going to be brought to bear to close this case, concluding it was a series of bear attacks, or some similar story. Billy Hatfield's death with be ruled a suicide, in all likelihood. You'll be pressured, and probably threatened, to forget the whole thing. They will demonstrate the means to discredit you, and then offer you a promotion, bonuses, a vacation, whatever they feel is appropriate to entice you, if you will only go along. I will be released from custody. If you did not know everything I had just told you, it might be enough to foster obsession. Madness, even. Lifelong doubts and fears you couldn't put into words. Men of more even temper than even yours have ended up hermits mailing bombs to 'Them' under such conditions. I have laid this out for you so you may, in time, accept it, and perhaps salvage your life. My advice? Go along. A monster was killed, the strain will be stemmed, and life will go on. I genuinely wish your good. This is why I tell you these things. Both of you."

There was a knock at the door of the interrogation room. It was Detective Sergeant Ingalls, and he looked grave when he gestured to them both that he would like a word. Father Giovanni lowered his head at this, looking down at his hands, again folded as if in prayer.

Frank leaned down to whisper to the priest as he passed him on the way out, "I don't roll over."

Father Giovanni replied, "Then, Heaven help you."

CHAPTER 34:
LELA MEETS ARIA

6pm
Wednesday
25 May, 2016

The Big Sur Public Library is little more than three rooms and a storage closet set among the trees and surrounded in the rear by a green lawn—all this just a few yards from Highway One. There is a low ramp with a rough-cut and unvarnished wooden railing that stands about chest high for Lela Crow. Inside and immediately to the left of the door is a community bulletin board, a children's area, and to the right is the double-duty Circulation and Reference desk. Across from that is Adult Fiction and against the opposite wall the only free wireless internet in Big Sur, two computers, and a heavy-duty copy machine/printer. To the right of this, an opening without a door to the nonfiction and poetry sections, as well as a small archival collection on Big Sur history and a small reading room on one side, and on the other is a community garden consisting of a handful of succulents and a bench out on an enclosed porch.

It could generally be staffed by one librarian, and that librarian was most often housed locally so as not to have to commute in each day over the winding highway cliffs from Carmel Valley or the Monterey Peninsula. Lela was glad that she had been called in to assist after the landslide had cut off Big Sur from the outside world. They needed her to step in so that coverage would not be interrupted when Mrs. Kinkaid, a woman of advancing years, might be able to enjoy her regular days off. The Big Sur Library had the only two public and internet-connected computers in the area, after all, and Lela felt it a duty to keep the lines of communication open for the now-stranded folk of Big Sur

This particular afternoon, Mrs. Kinkaid had gone home early, and Lela was alone when the rain began to patter on the flat roof of the library while gauzy grey light streamed in from the windows. There had been a handful of visitors that day, but the library was empty now and near silent. The clouds hung nearly low enough to be mist, and Lela stepped outside to regard the rain from under the eaves of the library.

What met her eyes when she opened the door made her gasp, but she did not draw back. The crows had returned in their hundreds, stooped and silent, crowding the railing. Some looked inward, toward her as she stood framed in the doorway, and others looked outward at what was to come. There was none of the usual hum from the grocer or the gas station or the roadhouse down the street, no one on the road. The place was eerily deserted, and for no reason she could name, Lela began to feel as if there were danger here, danger not because of the crows but prophesied by their presence.

That's when she saw a naked girl walking in the rain on the side of Highway One, weeping bitterly. Her cries and sobs were muted by the rain but were still audible to Lela. This girl was familiar somehow, but Lela could not place her.

She was slender, of pretty figure and face, tattooed about the arms and over the collarbones with various designs Lela could not quite make out. The girl, despite her weeping, looked dreamy, surreal, and she shivered in the rain walking toward the blinking sign of the roadhouse just around the corner: "Good Eats," it said.

By the time Lela locked the library and hung a laminated sign on the door ("Be Back Soon"), the girl had disappeared into the empty roadhouse. She hurried across the street, pulling on her black Pea Coat, and went into the roadhouse. She couldn't remember ever eating there, but it seemed to be open, unlike many of the other restaurants that had already begun to shut their doors for lack of meat and produce deliveries. She wondered as she stepped through the door where *Good Eats* got its meat.

A tall man in his late 50s was wrapping the girl in a fleece blanket when she came in. There was no one else in the place. He had close-cropped blonde hair that was peppered with gray, and he wore a red and black checkered flannel shirt over a close-fitting grey thermal shirt, both rolled to the man's thick-knotted forearms, some of which had some rather pronounced, if very old-looking, scars. He was broad-shouldered, broad-backed, and when he smiled up at her it was with very white teeth framed by rather pronounced canines.

"Hello," he said to Lela with cheerful good humor, "Do you know this girl? She doesn't seem to have much to say for herself."

"No, I mean, I don't think so. She just looked like she needed some help. Are you okay?"

The girl stared straight ahead, said nothing. Trembled. The big man eased her into a booth and said, "I'll get her some coffee. Any for you, ma'am?"

"Yes," said Lela, sitting down next to the near catatonic girl. "Coffee would be great. Thank you, sir."

"Sure thing," said the big man, "Call me Lorne." Outside, the rain intensified, pounding the black skin of the highway as darkness descended on the land.

CHAPTER 35

NOB MAKES A DEAL

3pm
Wednesday
May 25, 2016

ob had left Billy by mid-morning, intending to return after he had done what he never wanted to do. He needed to know where the *varulv* was that had infected the young writer, and this was a way, but Nob was afraid. He had stopped off at Roger Grimsby's house and picked up (although it had never been his custom and Roger was more than a little surprised) two tabs of LSD. Then Nob had gone back to *The Cauldron*. He pulled three books in particular from the shelves, locked the front door, dimmed the lights, poured a tall carafe of water and drank it down, refilled it, dropped the acid, and began the ritual.

The books Nob pulled down were entitled *The Chronicles of Fenrir: Exploring the Eschatology of Lupine Apotheosis* by Dr. Evelyn Patterson, Ph.D., a celebrated anthropologist; *Shape-Shifter: A Guide to the Spirit Ways* by Robert Iron-Heart, a Navajo shaman; and *Wards, Binding, and Protective Spells* by Belinda Woodleaf, a California spiritualist and Wiccan. He prepared a warding spell first, to ensure he would be protected, pouring a circle of salt out on the hardwood floor. He was dubious about how helpful it would be if it came to it, but Nob believed in observing the niceties.

He sat down cross-legged after he stripped off his shirt and pants. There he sat in his black boxer-briefs on the floor of the shop. He cut his hand, pouring his blood into a bowl. Then, he poured a measure of liquor into the bowl and a handful of herbs. He drank a measure of mead directly from the bottle. In the silence, he waited. Then, as he felt it coming over him, Nob began to whisper, "Speak with me," he said. "Grant me passage."

Outside, the sky began to darken. Thunder rolled. And Nob blinked out of reality.

Elsewhere (and when)…

The land was like Norway but not like Norway because if the fjords and highlands and the sea were dramatic in Norway, they were of another order of primal, elemental enormity here. The waves of the sea were as towers, and the highlands were enormous as the high thunderhead storm clouds are enormous, and Nob stood there dwarfed and gray in a land of such deep colors they threatened to unhinge his mortal mind in joy and weeping. There were no paths here, there was no sign of Man or Man's meddling. At Nob's back was a cliff to dwarf all cliffs in all nightmares for all time, a cliff so high and so far up over such a dark, frothing, thundering sea that it would have taken him days to fall if slipped from the edge. Upland to the east, a cave loomed like a mouth so enormous it might swallow a city. Nob began to climb. The rocks were jagged and razor-sharp. He cut his hands, his feet, knees, elbows, fingers, and toes, his chest and belly, and by the time he crested the rise just before the midnight opening of the great cave, the Moon, so large and full of pale light it filled his vision of the sky, had risen to silver every surface of the land.

Nob called into the cave, his voice echoing down and down and down into the very bones and foundations of Creation and the Spirit World, "Fen-Dweller, Monster of the River Van, Fenris-Wolf, Son of Loki! Speak with me! I am Nob, a Gothi of the Aesir, Favored of Crow and Raven, son of Aslaug Gothi of Odin. Will you speak with me, Fenris?"

Eyes of fire opened in the darkness of the cave, gargantuan as stars, and a wolf's head curled out from the gloom to be dusted by white-fingered moonlight. In his heart, Nob was afraid when The Great Wolf's Eyes fell on him.

"Speak, then," came the knee-jellying rumble of the Beast's voice, this Beast of all Beasts, this man-eater of all Man-Eaters, as deep and as powerful as the abrasion of continental plates.

"I come to learn of the wolves of Big Sur, by name and by history, and to learn how they may be stopped in their feeding and their spread."

"What do you offer?" snarled the Great Wolf, his breath like a fetid wind, icy as Arctic Winter from a frozen heart."

"Like Tyr before me, I offer my right hand."

"Your right hand is not the equal of Tyr's, little one," said Fenris.

"What would you have? I am no equal of the Aesir."

"I will have your Man's Shape. The doors and gates of Midgard are too small for even my least claw, anymore, but if you would offer your Man's Shape, I will give you all you ask."

Nob frowned, "I—I want to help stop the killing, and letting you wear my shape would not bring an end to killing, but bathe the land in blood. This I cannot do, O Great Wolf."

The impossibly great jaws arrayed with building-sized razor fangs yawned opened wide in a roar that found Nob trembling on his bloody knees in the scree.

"Then, I will eat you," said Fenris. "It's long since I devoured a Son of North Men."

The massive head began to drift toward him as tremendously-muscled shoulders rolled out of the dark of the cave.

A black cloud of Ravens descended calling and crying and screaming, "*Run, run run run run RUN!*" Nob turned, knowing it was futile, and began to run back down the hill whence he had come.

He fell, rose, fell again, sprinted, rolled down the hillside, dared not turn or look back as the winds whipped him into dull, faintly burning numbness. The sound of Fenrir behind him was the sound of an Arctic hurricane descending, like a god plummeting from the sky with a roar on its lips, like the Wolf of all Wolves coming on as sure as Death's own Scythe.

Finally, he came to the cliff's edge and turned, the crows and ravens swirled around him in a cloud, and there, with a grin of perfect hunger, loomed Fenris like a shadow. As huge as a mountain, the monstrous head descended to take Nob (and half the cliffside) into its jaws. The Crows called and the Ravens screamed and Nob closed his eyes, crossed his arms over his chest, and fell backward toward the sea. Fenrir roared in outrage and unrequited, famished hunger... but Nob felt that world-shattering roar through ears frozen and deafened by the salty, frigid winds. He sped downward toward the dark sea, and the crows and ravens swooped around him.

Give us your Man's Shape, and you will not die.

"What?" he said, his eyes opening to the dark birds who darted around him as he fell toward the green and frothing sea seemingly hundreds of miles beneath.

Give us your Man's Shape to wear, and we will give you our own.

Nob turned to regard the waves as big as skyscrapers far below him, felt the cold turning his skin grey. He knew he could fall for days and welcome Death when it finally came, alone in the Spirit World. What would come next? He dared not to contemplate it.

"Done," said Nob.

Done, screamed the crows.

Done, croaked the ravens.

They covered him suddenly like a shadow, like a dark cloud of feathers, and then he was gone... the dark mass of birds screamed and cried, and each winged off in his own direction, and the sky was empty but for that great Moon, and Fenris-Wolf sat on his haunches, silently silhouetted against it like a terrible mountain.

CHAPTER 36:

THE WOLVES OF BIG SUR

5pm
25 May, 2016

"Sarge, didn't expect to see you here," said Frank, as he stepped out of the interrogation room. Ingalls did not look happy.

"I hear you've got a priest in there," said Ingalls.

"That's right," said Frank, "We caught him with the gun in his hand, heard the report, and saw his body hit the floor."

"Did you see him pull the trigger?" asked Ingalls.

"No," said Frank.

"Right. Here's what happens next, Frank. You're going to cut him loose and apologize for taking up Father Santa Ana's valuable time. You're going to write up a report concluding that these homicides were the work of a rabid animal, probably a mountain lion, and then you're leaving Big Sur and starting your indefinite Leave of Absence."

"Excuse me, Sarge," said Frank, "but what the fuck are you talking about? A fucking mountain lion pulled out John Abrams' teeth one by one after carrying him upland half a mile without so much as a drop of blood, neatly removed his scalp, and then ate two bodies whole? A Mountain Lion removed and threw a car door into a cliffside at Bixby Creek Bridge? With all due respect, that's a load of horseshit."

Ingalls regarded Frank and said, "Look, Frank, if you don't want to write the report, you can go ahead and write me a resignation letter. I'll take your badge and gun right here and now. Push it, and you can go in for obstructing an investigation and tampering with evidence. Your intransigence and insubordination have gone on too long. You have disobeyed a number of my direct orders, refused to use modern communication to stay in touch with your chain of command, and you have delayed for days what should have been a simple investigation. Billy Hatfield was suicidal, and Father Santa Ana was there to talk him out of taking his own life. The pistol he used to take his own life was registered to Billy Hatfield, as a matter of fact. Meanwhile, this priest has friends in high places in Vatican City, Sacramento, and with the DOJ. You? You're fresh the fuck out of friends, Frank. So, what's it going to be? Your report? Or your early retirement and a night in gen pop at County?"

"Fuck you, Ingalls," said Frank with slowly rising Irish heat. "If you were half a man you'd step outside and settle it personally instead of hiding behind trumped up, cowardly traitorous yellow horseshit corruption. You make me fucking sick, and you're a goddamn disgrace. How's that for a fucking resignation, you piece of shit?" Frank slammed down his service pistol and badge on the desk beside where they stood as the deputies and Ranger Andy Parker stared on, mouths agape. Frank stalked out of the substation and into the pouring rain, and Ingalls hadn't enough spit in his mouth to tell him to stop.

When Father Giovanni stepped outside into the wet about ten minutes later, Frank, drenched and frowning, was leaning against his borrowed Park Ranger SUV, smoking his fifth cigarette since retirement. The priest went over to him.

"I respect your stand, Frank—" began the priest, just as Frank's fist connected with his jaw, and he went sprawling in the mud.

Giovanni stood, saying, "That one's free. I'm sure you're upset. I am not your enemy, Frank."

Frank shook his hand out, his knuckles bleeding. "You're going to go hunt down that girl? Going to kill her too, you fuck?"

"Yes, unfortunately" said the priest, "and the one who infected Mr. Hatfield."

"And then what? You think you and your Church can just make it all go away?" said Frank between clenched teeth.

"No," said Giovanni calmly even as his jaw was red and swollen and blood trickled from his lip, mingling with the rain, he regarded Frank almost sadly, "I'll go down one day, slower than some monster or other, and the war against evil will go on. I'm sorry it came to this pass, but this is the way it is. This is the world we were given to live in, and there is a price we all must pay."

"I want to see it," said Frank. "I *need* to see that this is real. That monsters exist. Not just their handiwork and not just a glimpse as they run out the back. Show me a goddamn werewolf."

Father Giovanni regarded him coldly, appraisingly, and then looked up at the storm and said, "You drive, then."

"Where?" asked Frank.

"Good Eats Roadhouse."

"By the library?" asked Frank.

"Yes, why?"

Frank skidded out of the lot and roared down the road.

Lorne had brought towels out of the back, and Lela had dried the girl's hair. Aria, who had still not spoken, finally stopped shivering after Lela managed to coax a little warm tea down her.

"We should call someone. My husband, maybe…" Lela said.

"Not much cell reception here," said Lorne. "But there's a payphone in the back. Go ahead and call."

She rose and turned a corner to the payphone by the restrooms, her footfalls strangely heavy on the unvarnished planks of the roadhouse. It looked like something out of a Route 66 diner, Lela thought, glancing idly at the Americana on the walls, the sawdust on the floor.

Lorne knelt beside their booth, his eyes on Aria's, his face close to hers. She felt somehow that she knew this man. There had been a fog after the change, and she had been drawn... *here*, to *him*... but she could not puzzle out why. The rational part of her brain was deep underneath, buried, clawing at an unmarked grave in the forest, screaming, screaming that she must not stay, screaming that this *thing* was wrong, this creature that wore a human face was more monster than she or Billy had ever been. A tear rolled down her otherwise impassive face as she sat in the booth, but she did not stir.

"The storm must have knocked the phones out," said Lela, coming back around the corner. "I guess we're out of luck and on our... own." She couldn't explain why she got a chill up her back to see Lorne crouched beside the booth where Lela slouched, as if whispering to her.

He looked up at her and his smile was friendly enough.

"Seems like that happens every time it rains hard around here. Probably some tree came down," he said. "To tell you the truth, I don't know. I grew up without a lot of the modern conveniences. Never bothers me to be without them."

"You should talk to my husband," she said. "He's the same way."

She pulled out her cell phone, but as Lorne had predicted, there was no reception. The rain redoubled itself, and now the windows were opaque with water and darkness. Again, she had the slightest feeling of danger but could not place it.

Lorne smiled toothily, "Oh, a man after my own heart."

"Yes," she said then changed the subject, a little uneasy. "Has she said anything?"

"Nothing, yet, but something scared her plenty," said Lorne. "Hey, have you eaten?"

"I had…"

a salad for lunch…

"…something a little earlier," she said, not entirely sure why, "I should—" But she wasn't sure what she should do. Go back to the Library? Probably no phone there either, and she felt sure she shouldn't leave this girl alone with Lorne, although he had been nothing but pleasant. And he was a local… surely she was just being paranoid. And yet…

"I have a great special tonight," he said, "Pork chops. My World Famous Pork Chops," he said with a strangely handsome smile. "Can I fix you something? Both of you? It's on the house."

No. No no no no. "Yes," she said, "Thanks. That sounds lovely."

His smile widened, almost alarmingly, and he nodded, moving gracefully back to the grill.

Aria reached out across the booth as Lela sat down, her eyes were cloudy, troubled, but unfocused. Lela draped her P-Coat around the girl, and said, "Are you hungry?"

Something primal bubbled up in Aria and manifested as a sudden terrible awareness flaring in her eyes. "Yes," she said in a strangely husky voice. "Hungry. *So hungry...*"

"She says she's hungry," said Lela, calling to Lorne's back across the counter and over the sound of the sizzling grill.

"Good," called Lorne back over his shoulder, "Very good. A good sign."

"What's your name, honey?" asked Lela.

"A-A-Ahhria," said the girl.

"Are you hurt?"

The girl shook her head. "P-priest. Bad priest. Sh-shot B-Billy…" Tears welled in her eyes.

"Someone was shot? By a priest?" asked Lela, her voice rising.

"Y-y-yeah," Aria said, her eyes far away again.

When Lela looked back in the direction of the grill, she nearly screamed to see Lorne looking at them both with unvarnished, malevolent glee verging and teetering on absolute homicidal madness. Like clouds across the moon, this expression was gone as quickly as it had come, and for a moment Lela wondered whether she had imagined it or not. When Lorne turned to mind the pork chops, which were just about done searing and ready to go into the oven, she reached into her purse and chambered a round in the 9mm pistol Frank had insisted she carry while they were in Big Sur. Aria seemed not to see her do it.

Lorne came around the counter after a few minutes and set down two plates of pork chops with all the trimmings. He set a dark bottle of wine on the table with two long-stem glasses.

"Isn't it usually white with pork?" she asked lightly, although she felt a knot rising from stomach to throat.

"This is something special," he said. "And believe me, it goes with the meal," said Lorne with a little chuckle, his voice struck her as deeper than it had been at first.

She looked up at him with a little smile. He looked just a little more hirsute than she had realized at first. His stubble was almost a light beard. His sideburns were thick, almost wooly, and his hair seemed longer than the crew cut. She was sure it had been a crew cut when she walked in.

"*Eat*," he said. Aria picked up her knife and fork, though Lela wanted to scream at her not to, and took a bite of pork chop, then smiled. Lorne, still looming over the table, poured her a glass of the red wine—it had a salty tang when Lela caught a whiff. Aria drank, sipping at first, then guzzling until it was gone. Lorne smiled on fiendishly as the girl began to eat with frenzied ap petite, grunting as she chewed, a wild look in her eyes.

"...*so* good," she breathed between bites, "so *juicy* and *good*."

Lorne's gaze felt like hot lamps on the flesh of her face. "You're not eating," he said.

Lela tried to respond, but no words could come. She felt like a rabbit under a tiger's paw.

"I—I'm... I need to use the restroom."

She made to stand, but he put his huge hand squarely and high on her chest and shoved her back into the seat. It was a light gesture, and yet she flew backward, her skull bouncing off of the Formica tabletop, splashing a thin line of blood across the white table.

"*I said eat*," said Lorne.

A car's headlights slid by in the rain and was gone around the corner, speeding off into the night. Aria had not looked up from her meal but had abandoned knife and fork and was licking the grease of the meat from the plate. Lorne smiled, tearing a piece of Lela's plated meat with his hand and feeding it to Aria as if she were a dog, she took it gratefully and licked his fingers for the juices when she had finished, then looked up at him pleadingly, "Please, I need more."

"Drink your wine," he said to Aria, who began to guzzle it directly from the bottle, whimpering in pleasure. He never broke his gaze away from Lela's, who was trying to clear her vision.

Had he been *so hairy* when she had walked in?? She was bleary now and thought she might have a concussion, but she was still reasonably sure he had been clean-shaven, or if not, then he had merely had the traces of five-o'clock shadow. But now he seemed to wear a dark gray beard that went up and down his neck and chest. He was smiling at her with *very* long teeth.

She went for her gun. But he must have been waiting for it because he lifted her by the throat and hurled her across the restaurant and against the far wall, snatching the gun away from her with his (claws?) other hand.

She felt a white hot wrenching and heard a wet, deep snap when he snatched the gun away. Her shoulder was probably dislocated and maybe broken, and she felt ribs crack when she hit the far wall and a wrist snap when she landed in a heap on the floor, breathless and struggling to gasp, her throat bruised where he had grabbed (clawed?) her.

She would have screamed to see him advance, but her vision was spotty, swimming, and strange, and besides she had no air in her lungs.

"I think I'll let this pup have you for seconds," he said evenly as he stood over her.

When Lela looked up, she saw Aria crawling on the floor, her face *elongated* horrifically, jaws slavering, and though her slender body was still recognizably human, it was sprouting fur and claws, and her eyes were growing luminous and terrible. Lela screamed then and thought she might go mad.

Aria was a wolf now, or a she-wolf anyway, seven feet tall and dark of hair and eye, her fur curled strangely where her tattoos rested beneath the skin, and her eyes were aflame with rage and hunger. She came on. Her mouth looked like an endless tunnel big enough to disgorge a train, lined with slavering, foaming jaws that champed and snapped like frozen pines in winter, or rifle reports in a tiny room. She leaped, and the arc of her descent was *wrong* somehow.

She landed on Lorne's back and began to tear at it and his neck with terrible strength and blinding fury. He shifted and threw her off, screaming in surprise and pain, bleeding a black ichor on the wooden boards that made them smoke and sizzle. He swiped at her and sent her reeling back against the wall, then he grasped her throat with both clawed hands and began to throttle her. His arms were so long, and even as she clawed at him her eyes were going dim.

Lela jumped up, crying out in the pain it brought on. She crossed the restaurant, limping as fast as she could. The terrible sounds of rending flesh and champing jaws and roars of anger and fear made her think of the lion house at the San Francisco Zoo when she was a little girl.

She got to the 9mm where it had been thrown near the front door and centered the monster's lower spine in her sights. She fired ten rounds in rapid succession— perhaps four of them connected, she wasn't sure. But Lorne had gone down, and now Aria had his throat in her jaws and was ripping, rending, tearing. He was clawing her neck open, ripping for her carotid artery, opening her eye like an overripe grape that spewed jelly all over the photograph of Jerry Lee Lewis on the wall beside them.

Lela grabbed her purse and fumbled for the second magazine Frank insisted on, and that's when a dark haired man in dark clothes burst through the door with a gun drawn and Frank beside him, holding a shotgun at the ready.

Frank nodded to her grimly but did not lose step with the dark man, who moved like mercury and smoke across the floor, silent and swift. He squeezed off a round, but Lorne lifted Aria's body as a shield, and she cried out in agony then went limp. The wolfman hurled the she-wolf at the two men; Frank dodged sideways into one of the booths, and Father Giovanni slid underneath, firing off another round, but the Beast wasn't where he had been—the double doors to the kitchen were swinging violently back and forth behind the back counter.

"Fucker's fast," said Frank, leaping over the counter and taking up a position by the door, ready for dynamic entry. The priest joined him.

Giovanni crossed into the kitchen on one side, Frank on the other. Lela hobbled over to Aria, who was still breathing shallowly, covered in blood, wheezing, and now herself again, a young girl, naked and trembling and dying on the floor of the roadhouse. Lela held her hand and wept.

"So, you believe me, then?" asked Giovanni.

"Not much choice," said Frank.

"We follow, and he doesn't get away," said Father Giovanni.

"Or we follow and die in the dark," said Frank.

"I'm going," said Father Giovanni, "stay with your wife."

Frank considered that a moment, then said, "No. This fucker is going down. Tonight."

Lela looked at her husband, stung beyond words. Frank tried to lean down, to begin to explain, but she recoiled.

"Your funeral," said Father Giovanni with a grin that didn't touch his eyes.

Frank stood erect and turned for the door. They cleared the kitchen, the back office, and found the backdoor swinging open on the stormy and very dark woods beyond, great five-toed wolf tracks, so familiar to Frank now, had left deep impressions in the mud.

The two men moved out quickly into the trees, expecting as soon as they hit the tree line that it would double back on its track. Each had a flashlight now, courtesy of Andy's Ranger SUV, and moved with measured, inexorable deliberateness deeper and deeper into the woods.

When they came to the Big Sur River, which was perhaps twenty feet wide and four feet deep there and of no great speed, the tracks disappeared. Frank cursed softly and turned a slow circle with the light across the bank and behind them.

A large river rock came whistling out of the darkness and crashed into Giovanni's hip from the opposite bank. He crumpled and said, "It's broken," with calm certainty.

Another rock came sailing out of the dark, even larger now, but Frank hooked arms with the priest and dragged him to the safety of a nearby tree. Then, as he straightened, the beast was on him, slashing upward and sending the shogun spiraling into the trees. It snapped at him, but he ducked low and shot left, rolling over a low boulder.

The priest shot Lorne through the stomach and the wolfman lurched back, making a sick churning sound like groaning steel before a building collapse. He slashed at Giovanni, but the priest had rolled away, broken hip and all, and his jaw was clamped down on a nearby stick, his face knotted in terrible pain, sweating fat beads of hot trembling ice down his forehead. Giovanni squeezed the trigger again and part of Lorne's shoulder disappeared. The Beast roared forward in rage and defiance and snapped the priest's neck as he bore all his weight down in the charge, then spun, somehow knowing Frank was there.

"Die!" Frank screamed, "Why won't you fucking die?" and fired five blasts into the wolfman's chest. The shots blew him backward into a tall pine and peppered him with black wounds. His blood visibly blackening and withering the tree as he slumped down and down. But the beast's wounds—except for those which had been made by the silver shot from Giovanni's gun, and which the silver had apparently passed through without striking anything instantly lethal—began to close.

Frank began to reload, now certain of death. Then there was a terrible sound in the sky, like a million crows ripping through a hole in reality, and a carpet of birds filled up every inch of the forest, the blackest concentration of which began to rip apart the screaming, roaring wolfman. In seconds, it seemed, they had flayed his flesh from his bones and rent him, in their thousands, into nothing. Their calls were the calls of madness, and the infinite, and of every charnel house and battlefield unto the ending of the world, a cacophony so limitless and so high it must have called down the very sky to witness, for lightning struck over and over in the trees around where Frank crouched in awestruck terror.

And then they were gone, along with any trace of Lorne Hutchins.

Frank limped back to find Aria seated on the floor, her wounds slowly closing and his wife beside her looking at him with strange, sad eyes.

CHAPTER 37

JUNE BRIDE

8pm
02 June, 2016

It didn't rain often, being summer in Monterey, but the rains had come again. Evening had darkened into night and still Lela sat at the bay window of the kitchen watching the driving water come down. She was cloaked in the silence she had carried like a garment of ice for the seven days since the death of Lorne Hutchins. Frank came through the door, his shift over, and halted as she ignored him.

"Hey," he said. He would have followed with, "are you okay?" but it caught in his throat.

She said nothing. Stared on at the rain.

"I, uh. I guess I'll go check on Aria upstairs. Is she healing up okay?"

"Remarkably," said Lela.

"And how about you?"

"Also, remarkably."

Frank tried not to and grimaced anyway. He didn't want to ask what it meant that she had healed so rapidly, as he knew she had—because he didn't want her to answer and because he already knew. He crossed the kitchen to head upstairs.

"I'm going to have to leave, Frank," Lela said. He froze mid-stride. He came around the kitchen table and sat beside her, took a breath.

"No," he said. "If this... if whatever this is... you and I will figure it out. We will adapt."

"That's the trouble. You're a Marine. A Detective. You think crises can be managed, and you're right. You think mysteries can be unraveled. And they can. But this isn't a crisis. It isn't a mystery. It's a curse. You can't ride out a curse."

"I don't believe in curses. I believe in us." Frank took her hand in his. She did not resist.

"If we ever make love again, it will pass to you. If I scratch you, or bite you, or lose control one night, you'll be cursed. If, God forbid, we have a baby..." she took a shuddering breath.

"So, we'll take precautions. We'll make a place for you to ride it out on those nights. We'll use protection in bed. You'll have to keep your nails trimmed," he tried to half-smirk. Her face remained a mask of sorrow.

"Please, Lela..."

"You almost died a week ago. Now you want to live with the thing that almost killed you?"

"You're not like that."

"Yes I am!" she said, standing and overturning the kitchen table with sudden hot rage. She turned and hurried up the stairs.

In the dark kitchen, Frank stood alone.

From above came the soft click as Lela locked Aria's bedroom door behind her, barely audible in that dark house over the whisper of rain.

To Be Continued in *Mani's Daughters*

Made in the USA
Monee, IL
31 January 2022

89657877R00146